Fatal Meeting

By

David O'Neil

Argus Enterprises International
New Jersey***North Carolina

A-Argus Better Book Publishers, LLC

For information:
A-Argus Better Book Publishers, LLC
9001 Ridge Hill Street
Kernersville, North Carolina 27285
www.a-argusbooks.com

ISBN: 978-0-6155350-3-6
ISBN: 0-6155350-3-8

Book Cover designed by Dubya

Printed in the United States of America

Chapter One

Donny decided he liked Abby. He was still pretty shy when he was around girls, but with Abby, he felt comfortable. That was the word, comfortable. She was someone that he could talk to, without feeling he had to prove his superiority. That was funny. Abby was the top in her class at the High School they both attended. There was no doubt in Donny's mind, who was the superior one, mentally at least.

Donny's position was comfortable, midway between average and top. He liked keeping a low profile, though not too low. Despite being well built, and fairly athletic, he was regarded as quite fit by most of the girls in his year. His quiet shy manner kept him in the background, when the more aggressive among the boys of his age were on the pull.

Abby had taken to the shy, nice-looking Donny, rather than the more boisterous and demanding, members of her age group. She did not take kindly to the assumption that a girl was a necessary accessory for any boy with status to maintain. Uncomfortable with the lewd suggestions swapped between many of the girls and boys around her, she suspected that in many cases the sex education classes that they all had to attend were in fact the basis for experiment by many who regarded their promiscuity as a status symbol. To Abby it was odd that the girl in 4th year, who was off school at the moment to have her baby, was regarded as some sort of heroine by her classmates.

They had met when she had bumped into Donny in the Friday Club, the early evening Disco dance held weekly in the Gym. Abby was taller than many in her year, one of the better-looking of her class; slim and athletic. She dressed without emphasizing her femininity with the padded uplift bras and the pelmet skirts of some. Nor did she wear the skimpy tops and low-cut jeans so many of the others wore that showed expanses of flesh often bisected with the T of their thong underwear. Tonight she was wearing a crisp pale blue blouse with a just-above-knee length navy skirt that flared slightly.

She had swung away from the snack bar with a cup of coffee in her hand and bumped into Donny who was behind her. "Whoops, sorry! Nearly had an accident."

"No problem." Donny grinned "That's a bit full. Perhaps you'd better sit down somewhere with all this mob about." He indicated the crowded dance floor and, noticing her juggling with her slipping shoulder bag, a cup, plus a paper plate with a cake on it, said. "Hang on. I'll take that." He took the plate and cup, and turned and strode over to a bench and table where there was room to sit. Putting the cup and plate down, he said, "Back in a minute." And dashed over to the bar and collected a coffee for himself.

Abby had seated herself on the bench, bag beside her not quite sure how she had found herself sharing her coffee break with a boy.

Donny joined her on the bench, coffee in hand. He smiled at her and said "You're Abby Marshall, aren't you? I'm Donny Weston."

"Yes, I know." Abby said "You play basketball for the school, don't you?"

"And you play netball for the school. Am I right?" He looked at her directly and she found herself blushing. She noticed that he had a red tinge too and realized that he was also blushing.

Both sipped their coffee and both started to say something simultaneously. Both stopped. Then the same thing happened. Abby broke the cycle, "You first."

"I'm sorry. I'm not used to talking to girls. I suppose I'm at a loss. I don't really know what to say."

Abby looked at him searchingly, then "Try saying what comes into your head without attempting to be smart or witty. Don't worry about it. Just say something you mean." She found herself holding her breath waiting to hear what he would come out with.

Donny thought for a moment then decided to do just that. "I was trying not to say that I have been trying to pluck up the courage to speak to you all term. I know you're pretty brainy and I can see you are attractive. I've wanted to speak to you and find out if what I see is what you are really like. Or words to that effect." He started to get up, "So, if I've upset you, I'm so...."

She reached out and took his arm. "Where are you going? You don't think I'm going to let you go without a chance of a reply, do you?"

Confused he sat down. He had convinced himself that she would put him off after that little speech. He was leaving before he got too embarrassed.

Without taking her hand from his arm, as if to make sure he didn't run away, Abby looked at him seriously for a moment. Then she smiled, "What was that all about?"

"Well, you said to say exactly what was on my mind. I thought you're right. it is best to be honest up front sometimes and that this might be the only chance I would get. So I'd better make the most of it." The grin was shamefaced, but it was also without guile.

"Did you mean what you said just now?"

"Of course I did. What do you take me for?" The indignant tone said it all.

"You're serious? You want me to be your girlfriend?" Abby blushed as she said this. The only other time she had consented to be someone's girlfriend she had finished up on the first date fighting off his groping hands that were attempting to undo her brassiere. The left hook backed by the muscle of her goal-scoring arm finished the struggle by giving her escort a bleeding nose and a serious complex about his manhood.

"Of course I do. Will you?"

To her surprise, and Donny's, she said, "I...I think I would like that."

Donny said nothing. He just took her hands in his across the table. He looked her straight in the eye and said "Good."

He was red-faced as he continued. "I wanted to ask you the first day you came to our school, when we were both fourth formers. Then you went out with that idiot Patrick. I thought that was it, all over for me. He always seemed to get the girls. When you dumped him the next day I thought if he couldn't keep you, what chance would I have. One thing led to another. I was disgusted when that girl Shirley got pregnant. I thought girls had to be pretty rough to do things like that at her age. Most of the other girls seemed to be having sex with their boyfriends. At the time I got pretty disgusted with the whole girl-boy business.

"Eventually I decided I was being silly. It was quite obvious that not all the girls were like that. You hadn't carried on with any of the others. I got the impression that you had decided to get on with your work and you seemed to withdraw from the people around you. I guess I thought you had cut boys out of your life while you studied. So I stood back and yearned from afar." He finished with a giggle that took the sting out of his comment.

"Okay, not a bad summing up. Let's start again. I'm Abby. How do you do? Will you be my friend?"

"Donny's the name, and Abby, I would love to be your friend."

They shook hands like two strangers meeting and the deal was struck.

* * *

The countryside was magical that summer. For some reason the specter of 'Global Warming' had not been able to cast a blight on the series of fine summer days. Donny introduced Abby to the joys of sailing, initially in his own dinghy.

Christchurch had been the ideal spot to teach her. Then after he had been convinced that she had grasped the rudiments of boat handling, they stepped up to his father's 40ft ketch *Swallow*, the Elizabethan Class yacht with a deep keel and impeccable manners. She was kept at Parkstone on a mooring. Provided the tide was right they were able to sail off the mooring without too much effort. Usually they went with Donny's dad. Sometimes, when he couldn't manage to go, he would ask Peter

Davey to go with them. Peter was the man who did any jobs on the boat for Mr. Weston and any other of the owners in the area. He was a quiet man in his late twenties. Donny thought he was odd, but harmless.

The run up to the summer holidays was occupied with the pair learning to sail the boat together as a team, and getting to know each other.

The possibility of taking the *Swallow* over to Brittany and down the coast to an overwinter berth in La Rochelle had been touched upon. It became very much a case of convincing Donny's father that they were up to it. From Donny's home in Ringwood access to Christchurch for the dinghy sailing and to Parkstone to sail the Ketch, was comparatively easy. Donny had a motorbike and he could pick up Abby from her home in Poole whichever way they intended going.

During those first weeks both had to adjust to having, for the first time in their lives, someone to talk to and confide in. It seemed they both were prepared to wait and see how things developed. Neither felt any pressure to rush matters. Because of this they became good friends from the very beginning.

Abby's mother, Mrs.. Marshall, was a widow. Abby's father had been killed in Afghanistan. He had been a Flight Lieutenant in the RAF, flying

Helicopters. He had been shot down and killed in the crash, having served six months in the country.

Donny got the whole story when he questioned the picture on the sideboard in Abby's home. He had assumed her lack of a father at home was down to the usual reason among most of the kids at school, divorce. In his own case his mother and father were still together after 24 years, and they were showing no signs of parting. His father was partner in a law practice he shared with his brother. Donny's older brother, Michael, was articled to the firm, having gained his LLB at Sussex University.

Abby enjoyed visiting the Weston house. She was always made welcome. The family had reacted to the alliance between Abby and Donny with genuine pleasure. The fact that they were such good friends was obvious. They all treated her like the daughter they never had.

As the summer holiday loomed nearer, it was Abby who brought the subject up when the entire family were seated in the Conservatory, watching the rain fall after a long hot spell.

She spoke to the group at large, almost offhand. "When do you plan on taking the *Swallow* down to La Rochelle?"

Mr. Weston yawned and said, "When you've both finished with your exams I thought you could take her over to Cherbourg with Peter Davey." Once you are there and moored up, Peter can get the ferry back. If I can't get away immediately you could have a snoop around the Cherbourg Peninsula for a day or so. I can get the ferry across overnight and join you in the morning. How does that sound?"

Donny looked at Abby. In unison they said, "Fine."

Abby said to Mrs.. Weston, "Will you be coming with us?"

"I'm sorry, dear. I would like to but I'm stuck with organizing the WI sale and a stall at the local summer show. I'm hoping that I'll be able to join you later in the summer for the cruise down to Bordeaux and the North Spanish coast."

"So there we are, all arranged no bother, pas de problemo," was the way Dan Weston put it. Abby hugged Mr. Weston, excited at the prospect. Then she and Donny got kitted out to return to her home.

The house was quiet and empty when they arrived. There was a note on the kitchen table. 'Abby and D, There is a casserole in the oven, just serve up two plates and stick them in the micro. See you about 9.00, Love, Ma.'

Having eaten, they went through to the lounge and lay on the floor watching TV. Abby shifted over and rested her head on Donny's shoulder. "You don't mind, do you? I'm getting a stiff neck on that cushion. Donny slipped his arm round her and gave her a hug. "Comfortable?"

"Yes." The word came out like a sigh and Abby dropped off to sleep.

* * *

"Wake up you two. Donny needs to get home, you know." Mrs.. Marshall's voice brought them back to life in a hurry.

"Wow, it is nine o'clock already. Abby said "You'd better get a move on."

Donny rushed out to the kitchen to get his gear on. He got a hasty kiss from both of them and left them standing on the step waving him off.

* * *

The days passed all too slowly that term. The rest of the class realized that Donny and Abby were an item and in the main left them to it. But there is always one. This was a boy called Roger Harris. He was not popular and he was a bully. He decided that the quiet couple would be an interesting target for his interest. He fancied Abby and thought he had chosen his moment when she would be alone. He had a thing about the short skirts and white blouses worn by the netball team. After netball he had noticed that Abby always changed her clothes rather than leaving it until she got home like most of the others. Netball was in the final periods of the afternoon.

Stationing himself outside the pavilion chang-ing rooms he counted the girls who went in and came out. He worked out that Abby would be alone and carefully opened the door.

Donny came round the corner in time to see Roger's back as he passed through the door. He heard the key click in the lock and realized what was happening. He ran quietly round the Pavilion to the front door and slipped in. There were voices coming from the changing rooms.

Inching open the door, he slipped into the vestibule and peered through the glass into the locker room.

Abby stood defiantly in bra and pants with her blouse in her hands. Roger was leering at her from the far entry. "Don't bother dressing for me, darlin'. I prefer you with your clothes off."

"Get out of here, you disgusting little oik." Abby was not about to knuckle under to him.

Roger grinned nastily and stepped forward reaching out to grab her.

Donny stepped through the door at the other end of the room. "Anything I can do, Abby?" he said quietly.

Roger froze on the spot. This was not supposed to happen in his scenario.

Abby slipped the blouse on, watching Roger like a hawk. She was worried about Donny because Roger was a big lad. He looked dangerous to her. She carried on dressing while Donny walked forward to stand between Abby and Roger.

Worried, Abby said. "Don't hurt him. The poor lad is probably weak in the head coming into the ladies' changing room like this."

Roger laughed. "You gotta be kidding. This little wimp couldn't swat a fly." He reached forward to cuff Donny round the face.

Donny grabbed the hand and wrenched it, swinging Roger round, thrusting his hand up his back forcing it between his shoulder blades.

"Here stop it. What...ouch.. let go.. You'll break my arm." This last was a whine.

"Listen to me, you disgusting toe rag. I'm being gentle with you because the lady asked me not to hurt you. I'll make this short and sweet. If I come across you insulting or threatening a woman again, I'll beat you so badly you will beg me on your knees to stop. I don't like bullies, and bullies who threaten violence to my friends cause me to lose my temper. Am I getting through to you?" He jerked the hand a little more to emphasize his comment.

"I get it. I understand. Now please let me go."

Donny let go and turned to Abby, "Whenever you're ready."

He saw the look of horror on her face and dropped to his knees. The hockey stick whipped past his head as it swung in a vicious blow that would have seriously injured him.

He didn't wait this time. Springing to his feet he lashed out at the unbalanced Roger, hitting him hard on his jaw beside his ear.

The bully crashed to the floor, breaking one of the benches by the wall. Donny gripped him by the lapels and wrenched him to his feet. Roger was sobbing in pain. There was dribble from his half-open mouth. His nose was leaking blood where he had hit the broken bench.

"My patience is being stretched by your silly boy games. There will be a notice on the notice board in the school lobby when you leave. It will explain that you fell on the bench and it broke. It will also say you are sorry. And that you will pay for its repair. Nod, if you understand me." He waited while the battered boy nodded.

"If there is any comment about what happened here, regardless of how it happens, I will hurt you. No more games like today or I will seriously cause you pain." He dropped his hands. Leaving the boy swaying gently and still crying, he took Abby by the hand and they left the ladies changing room.

Chapter Two

Abby was taken aback. "I thought you were going to get clobbered by him when you came in. Don't get me wrong. I was never more pleased in my life when you walked through the door. How did you know?"

"I saw him sneaking in through the other door and I heard him lock it. So I dashed round the front. You know the rest." He was still trembling inside in reaction. He wasn't sure whether it was elation or terror. He was happy that he had come out of his first fight in one piece. He now appreciated the training program that had concentrated on self discipline. It included unarmed combat techniques that gave them the practice in exercising their discipline. As their instructor had stressed more battles and contests are won with discipline than with enthusiasm. He had continued performing the exercises when he was selected for the basketball team simply because it seemed the easiest way to keep fit.

Abby said "He won't tackle you again, not after that little episode. I'm so proud of the way you stood up to him. After all he is bigger than you."

"He was going to attack you. He said so. I couldn't allow that. I was just lucky, I guess. It was you that warned me about the hockey stick." He squeezed her arm under his and the subject was dropped.

* * *

It did come up again however. When Abby was visiting the house at the weekend, they were both studying for their final 'A' levels that would mark the end of their schooldays. Both were intending going to University next year.

Donny winced as he knocked his knuckle against a chair leg. They were lying side-by-side on the floor posing questions to each other. Abby saw him and said, "I bet Roger hurts more than you do."

"Who is Roger? And why should he hurt more than you? Have you been fighting?"

His father's voice came from the armchair in the corner. Neither of them was aware he had come in and settled down with a book.

"You'd better tell me all about it, young man. Just in case I have to defend you on a charge of assault." Mr. Weston sounded and was, quite serious.

So Abby rolled over, faced Mr. Weston and told him the story without any embellishment.

"Did the note appear on the Notice Board?" He asked.

"It certainly did." Abby replied.

Donny was keeping his head down pretending to concentrate on his books.

Mr. Weston got out of his chair and sat down in front of them both. "This is the first time I have heard of Donald getting mixed up in rough stuff. He smiled "I'm proud of you, son. Whilst I'm also proud that you kept the whole business to yourself, in this day and age it might be better if you let me know in future if anything like this happens. Society today has gone crazy. People sue at the drop of a hat. I know you won't seek trouble. But if it comes along just keep me in the loop, if you know what I mean." He ruffled Donny's hair and returned to his book.

* * *

The Ketch was a pleasure to sail. With a crew of three there was no real problem handling the sails. The fore was roller-reefed, thus already hoist. The main was hoisted with a hand winch that Abby could handle on her own. The Mizzen was winch-hoisted but Peter Davey hoisted it by hand to save bother and reeled the winch afterwards. They had motored out of Poole Harbour, waving to the people on the sundrenched Shell beach.

As the bow lifted to the swell of the open channel waters Donny's heart seemed ready to burst with the joy of being at sea once more. From the wheel he could see Abby in skimpy shorts and a knotted blouse, tidying up the sheets from the newly hoisted sails, laughing as the spray showered her from the dipping bow. Peter was below preparing coffee and sandwiches for lunch. They would cook for the evening meal. During the day they would take things easy until they had shaken down together. On the cabin roof in front of him lay the folded dinghy Peter had brought to save them unshipping the tender attached to the davit over the stern of the boat. Donny had suggested that they were quite happy to use the tender. Peter insisted he would rather be independent. Peter was in a stubborn mood. When he was like that it was pointless arguing.

Abby had suggested that they could have managed on their own. Peter was such a dour man that he sometimes cast a pall on the party, even when the others were there.

It was all to no avail. Mr. Weston was insistent that the passage across the Channel where there were so many major ocean routes to cross the extra pair of eyes was important and that was that.

Finished with cleaning up Abby went below and fetched coffee for Donny and herself and joined him in the cockpit.

With the sun warm on their faces one second, hidden in the shadow of the sails the next, they whiled away the hours of Donny's spell on the wheel happily.

The wind was steady from the west and the boat made good steady progress on course to Cherbourg. They all ate the corned beef sandwiches prepared by Peter. Donny handed the wheel over to Peter while he and Abby stretched out to enjoy the sunshine.

Abby could not help noticing Donny had developed physically over the months she had known him. He had always been well toned and smooth-muscled. His basketball activities had made sure of that. But now he had filled out more over the shoulders. With his trim waistline he could be called a hunk. He had a good face, not handsome as such, but with regular features and smiling eyes. *Hazel,* she thought. *Yes, hazel and with fair hair, bleached by the sun. Yes.* She decided a little mental 'Grrrrr' was merited.

Donny turned his head at that point. "What are you thinking about so quietly?"

"Oh, nothing. You know; this and that."

"I don't know. What's this and that?"

"Just day dreaming, if you must know."

"Looking forward to Cherbourg?" He smiled at her. "I am."

"I'm looking forward to losing Old Gloomy there." She nodded her head at Peter who sat stolidly in the cockpit twenty feet away from where they were laid out, steering the boat with a surprisingly delicate touch.

"Oh, Peter's not so bad. He's a good helmsman and crew in the boat."

"Whatever he is, he gives me the creeps."

"You and Mum both. I think that's why she arranged the WI thing for now. She doesn't enjoy sailing with him along. Never has." Donny's voice expressed his puzzlement over this. "Strange. It's always the women who are uncomfortable around him, never the men."

"He doesn't radiate lust, like some men; almost the opposite. It's as if he doesn't see us, as women, I mean. As if for him we don't exist." She saw the look Donny was giving her. "Oh I don't mean he's homosexual. It's more like asexual if you know what I mean."

"Okay. Lady Macbeth." Donny rolled over and nudged her in the ribs. "You've only got to survive his presence until Cherbourg, about nine more hours. Then he will be gone. We will have the boat to ourselves for at least twenty-four hours till Dad comes. So we'll just have to grin and bear it, suffering this lazy period lying about in the sun doing nothing." He rolled back and sprawled out again with a sigh.

Abby leaned over and gave him a kiss on the lips. "Thank you, kind sir, for being my friend and bringing me on this luxury cruise." She returned to her place.

She just heard him whisper "Keep that up. I could get addicted to this."

She smiled to herself. Things were working out just as she had hoped they would. She dropped off to sleep in the warm sunlight.

* * *

The evening meal was easy to prepare. Mrs. Weston had prepared stew, sealed in a Tupperware container for the voyage. All Abby had to do was to heat it up and serve it with the crusty bread from the local bakery in Ringwood.

Now pumped up, Peter's inflatable dinghy was at present bobbing along in the wake behind them. Peter said that it would save him disturbing everyone in the dark when he left in the early morning. Donny pointed out that it would be light anyway. But Peter was Peter and that was that.

After clearing up the dishes Abby took the early watch. They had agreed it was sense to keep a physical watch crossing the shipping lanes in the Channel at night. Peter was scheduled for the midnight watch from ten pm to two am. By then the lanes would be passed. Then Donny would do the two am to six am that would bring them into Cherbourg and their mooring.

The two youngsters slept in the bunks in the saloon. It was convenient. Peter used the after double cabin. The fore cabin, which was also a double, was in use for the luggage for the onward journey from

Cherbourg. Donny kept Abby company during her watch, bringing her a fleece when the night grew chill after the warm day. The starry night was a suitably romantic background for the couple who cuddled together and enjoyed their private moment.

When Peter came to relieve Abby at the wheel he brought them both mugs of cocoa. "To help you sleep," he said, and smiled.

Below Donny put his mug on the sink while he helped Abby get her sleeping bag organized. After drinking her cocoa she received a hug and a kiss and a sleepy goodnight. He turned to sort out his own sleeping bag and knocked his mug into the sink.

"Sod it!" He said ruefully looking at the sludge of brown liquid as it ran down the plughole. With a shrug he washed the two mugs and hung them on their captive hooks, taking a drink of water he climbed into his sleeping bag and dropped off to sleep.

He was not aware of why he woke when he did. He looked at his watch and realized he was late for his watch. When he climbed out of the bunk he smelled gas. Donny was an experienced sailor, having sailed with his father for many years. He went straight to the stern locker in the cockpit and shut off the supply. Then back into the fore cabin where he opened the fore hatch.

The through draught shifted the gas in the boat in a hurry. To be sure he turned on the shielded gas detector and pump that was designed to flush out the bilges of any gas laying there.

He checked Abby. She was breathing heavily. He shook her trying to waken her, but she just lay there refusing to wake up. Danny lifted her up and carried her in her sleeping bag into the cockpit where he made sure that the air she was breathing would be free of any residual gas.

Then he looked about for Peter. The towed dinghy was gone. As he scanned the area he caught a glimpse of a light off across the waves. He snatched up the glasses and focused on the area. There it was again outlined in the cone of a torch, the dinghy and another boat. He could not make out the lines of the other boat. But he could see the dinghy being hauled aboard.

Abby seemed alright apart from the deep sleep. So Donny went below and checked the gas lines from the tank to the stove. There was a fracture. The teeth marks of the pliers were visible in the copper of the tubing. A section two inches long had been removed. He searched the other line to the heater. There were no other breaks. He went out and checked on Abby once more. She was still breathing steadily and seemed alright. If he had not woken when he had, they would both probably be dead by now.

Donny's fright had turned to anger. What about Abby and himself? Peter must have planned this. Or at least been part of the scheme whatever it was. He went to the toolkit and pulled out a piece of screened plastic tubing and cut it to size. He then slipped it onto the cut ends of the gas pipe, anchoring it firmly with two banjo clips one at each end. The self-steering was still keeping the yacht on course. Having checked the heading Donny started the engine. The lights of Cherbourg were in sight but there was still an hour to go.

Abby had not stirred but was still breathing evenly. Donny was worried that the people who were trying to blow up the boat would be following them to make sure that they were destroyed as planned.

It was then he had the idea. He switched on the ship to shore radio and turned to the distress frequency, "Mayday. Mayday. Mayday." he called "This is the Ketch *Swallow* en route to Cherbourg from Poole. We have lost a man overboard." He gave the GPS location. "Can we have assistance. Please. Over."

The Cherbourg radio answer was immediate, "Ketch *Swallow,* maintain your position. Help is on the way. Do you need any assistance with your boat? Over."

"Hullo, Cherbourg. This is Ketch *Swallow.* We are fine and safe. But we have lost our crewman

Peter Davey who was on watch over midnight. I discovered he was missing when I went to relieve him. Over."

The roar of a helicopter and the seeking cone of light from it highlighted the boat. Donny caught a glimpse of the other boat in the backwash of light sweeping over the waters around the *Swallow*. The other boat was a sloop, perhaps 60 foot, dark hull and blue sails.

Her lights suddenly came on. A loud hailer clicked on with an electronic squeal and a voice called across the water. "Sorry about that. We lost power and the lights went out. The cut-out jammed and we've just cleared it. We had you on radar on a different circuit and were bringing your man back to you, when we picked up your mayday. If you'll stop for a moment we'll float him down to you in his dinghy."

Under the glaring eye of the helicopter Donny cut the engine and brought the boat up to the wind. The stranger launched the rubber dinghy. Peter got in and was allowed to drift on the end of a line to the stopped *Swallow*. Donny hauled the dinghy in and took the released rope from the other boat, tying the dinghy off behind. Cupping his hands he called "Thanks," to the other boat. It turned away immediately. But not before Donny had seen the name on the stern, *Dorney* Newhaven.

He turned to Peter. "Call Cherbourg and tell them 'thanks' for the help. You have been found unhurt. Now!"

Without a word Peter stepped past the recumbent figure of Abby, picked up the radio mike and called Cherbourg.

* * *

Abby woke as the mooring was being hooked on by Donny. Peter was gone. He had rowed ashore as they entered the harbor. She raised her head from the depths of her sleeping bag and peered muzzily round. Donny came back and joined her in the cockpit.

"Hi there, sleepyhead. How are you feeling now?"

"What happened last night? I dropped off to sleep in my bunk. I wake up in the cockpit. So what's up?"

Donny told her about last night, and what he had done. "I still don't know what it was all about."

While Abby climbed out of her sleeping bag Donny got the papers together to present to the Harbormaster and Customs.

They went ashore together. Having cleared the boat they went shopping in the big Hypermarket. Donny spoke to his father, being careful not to mention Peter Davey's part in the events of the night. Davey's story was that he had stepped into the dinghy to make sure that all was packed and ready. The painter came adrift He was left drifting in the open waters of the Channel.

They got back to the *Swallow* after lunch in one of the waterfront restaurants. Having put the shopping away they transferred the luggage from the forward cabin to the after cabin used by Peter on the way across. Once cleared, they crashed on to the big double bed. They lay there side by side for some time, before Donny finally spoke. "I thought for a moment that bastard had killed you. When I realized that he had only put you to sleep for a while, I decided he could live.

Abby asked the question that Donny had been dreading. "But why did he drug me and try to drug you. What good would it do? For him, I mean."

Donny decided he had better tell the whole story. When he finished Abby looked at him and said. "You saved my life."

He said "Well, mine too. And don't forget Dad's boat."

She reached out to him and pulled him to her. They kissed passionately, really passionately for the first time.

The restraint they had exercised for the past months melted away as they removed their clothes and clung to each other for the first time, discovering and joining together as lovers. They had both known this would happen when the time was right. Neither had any intention of rushing things. Having shared a near death experience, it seemed to be the right time for them both. Later, as they surveyed the wreckage of the bedclothes following their first amateurish excursion into lovemaking, Abby, ever practical, said, "We can buy more sheets at the Hypermarket before your dad arrives."

Donny grinned "Most people, even those who know us well, would never believe that we waited so long. Did we do the right thing?"

"You silly man, of course we did. Most of our friends started with a grope up some back alley, or at least on the back seat of the car. We can look back and say at least 'we started the way we mean to go on'." She looked anxious for a moment. "We will be going on, won't we?"

Astonished, Donny looked at her open-mouthed. "I don't think it's meant to be a one off." He said, equally anxious."Is it?"

They stood looking at each other for a moment. Then burst out laughing and fell on the bed, still naked and happy at the closeness between them.

Chapter Three

The message came that evening from Donny's father. Either they would have to wait in Cherbourg for another day, or, if they were happy with the weather, they could take the boat round to Granville for two nights. They could meet him from the Channel Islands ferry.

Donny told his father that they would sail for Granville after tomorrow and only spend one night there, as they had to report to the Police Station in the morning. Peter Davey had been found mugged and killed in the town overnight. He was known to have come from their boat. Donny had been asked to identify the victim.

"Do you know anything about it?"

"Not really."

"What does that mean, not really?"

"I would rather not speak about it on the phone. I'll tell you when you arrive. Meanwhile I promised to let you know if anything iffy happened, so I'm letting you know."

After another few comments he switched the phone off and turned to Abby. We'll see him in two days time. Meanwhile we still have some time alone together. He turned her to face him and took her into his arms. "I have felt this way ever since we got together. The more I got to know you the surer

I became. I love you, Abby Marshall. When the time comes I want to marry you and spend the rest of my life with you."

Abby looked up at him "Good. The only thing is.... now I'll never know what life would have been like without you." The tears ran down her cheeks and she drew his head down and kissed him.

There was a little stiffness between them after this revelation. The atmosphere eased as they became a little less embarrassed over their mutual declarations.

After eating and clearing up they both felt drained by the events of the past two days. They looked at the later news on the TV but nothing new came up.

Donny thought for a while. Then said seriously, "We have a serious problem. Now Peter is dead the villains know who we are. We have no idea who they are, and more importantly, what they want. The reason I mention it is that you should know about the Weston hole card."

"What are you talking about, the 'Weston hole card'?"

They were sitting on the port bunk in the saloon. It doubled as a seat during the day. He leaned across to the starboard side and rotated two of the curtain rod holders. They carried the curtain that could be pulled round the bunk for privacy, or to keep the light out for watch-keepers resting during the daylight hours. The roof panel above the berth dropped revealing a rack of guns. There were four automatics and two Armalite semi-automatic rifles. Beside each weapon was a block of four magazines. Donny took one of each, a rifle and an automatic pistol down from the rack and closed it once more.

"Dad and Grandad brought the *Swallow* up from Durban in South Africa via the Suez Canal. There was trouble in Tanganyika and Zanzibar and the Ethiopia/Eritrea areas plus problems in Yemen and Aden. They decided that they would need to be prepared for anything, since pirates have always operated on that coast as well. Granddad had this panel fitted in the boatyard before they left Durban.

"I'm told that they had a running battle with an unknown dhow off Zanzibar. They were actually both wounded in a skirmish further north with Yemeni so-called fishermen."

As he told the story he checked that the guns were empty and passed the pistol to Abby. He showed her how the magazine slotted into the butt and the action cocked. He also stressed that the safety catch had to be released before the gun would fire.

He also showed her the rifle and pointed out its salient points. "When we are alone at sea I'll teach you to shoot. We just have no idea what will happen next. Whatever happens we will try to be prepared. After all Peter worked for them and they killed him."

Abby handled the guns determinedly. "I understand what you are saying, but aren't these guns illegal?"

"In fact, no. As a seagoing yacht that travels to parts of the world where pirate activity occurs, licenses are available, provided security is provided for the weapons.

* * *

The visit to the police headquarters was not a pleasant experience. Donny insisted that he would go alone to identify Peter's body. The stab wounds were not apparent so the identity was a matter of the simple exposure of the face. Donny thought that Peter looked more at peace than he had ever seen him. The perpetual dour look was no longer apparent. As the sheet was pulled up once more it occurred to him that whatever had been the cause of Peter's eternal discontent was now resolved.

He made a statement to the officer identifying the body as Peter Davey, who had left the boat to return to England yesterday morning.

The *Swallow* left her mooring later that morning, neither of the young people having much to say, despite the bright sunshine and the fresh breeze.

* * *

The crack of the shot was louder than she expected. She flinched. The bullet missed the floating target by a yard. Donny adjusted the position of her arm, pushing it firmly into her side. "Now, point your finger at the target. She swung her hand round keeping her wrist firm, the pistol in line with her forearm. As soon as she thought she was lined up she squeezed the trigger once more. The plastic float jumped as the bullet clipped the edge.

Donny turned her partially toward him and kissed her quickly, then swung her back. "Now do it again," he said.

Despite the distraction she lined her arm up with the target and fired once more. The bullet flicked the water in front of the target.

"Good enough for just now." Donny was well pleased. Abby had got the message. She could at least, as he put it, scare the hell out of someone with the gun.

He let out the rope tied to the target float, extending the range from about twenty feet to ten fathom mark on the line. He considered 60 feet suitable as a start with the rifle.

Shooting a rifle from a swaying boat is difficult at the best of times. For someone who has never used a rifle before it is asking a lot. The timing is all about anticipation, taking into account where the target is going to be when the bullet arrives. Skeet shooters, duck hunters and game hunters know all about it. To the best it's pure instinct. You either have it or you don't.

Abby had it. Her first shot went astray when she misjudged the trigger pressure required. From then on she astonished Donny, and delighted herself, by placing six shots from the semi automatic rifle into the float. By so doing, she ruined the float for future use, but demonstrated that the Armalite was hers. The rifle had little kick because the main force was absorbed in the reloading of the chamber.

"I did it. I did it." she turned to Donny, who hastily took the rifle from her before allowing her to hug him in delight.

Donny grinned at her, then removed the magazine and called her to collect the spent cartridges from the deck where they had been ejected. He counted them all to make sure they had missed none then threw them overboard.

They both surveyed the horizon all round the boat. There were two ferries in sight in the distance, passing between Portsmouth and Guernsey. On the landward side the headland of Cap de la Hague lay astern, in the haze. The loom of the Channel Islands, overlapping and appearing almost of being one piece of land, lay off to the west, also in the haze. The fresh breeze that had brought them this far had dropped to light fluky airs. To Donny that meant a change in the weather.

They were still making headway but he was not too sure how long that would last. Making the decision, he decided to shorten sail and he called Abby to lower the main. Setting the self-steering he went to help handling the sail. They folded it over the boom and lashed the ties to keep it in place. He reefed the mizzen down to a quarter size, leaving the foresail full for the moment. Though the boat was slightly unbalanced, he put Abby on the wheel while he started the engine.

Back in the cockpit once more he started to reel in the foresail, feeling the boat's movements until the balance felt right. With about a quarter of the foresail now set the boat rode easily. Donny let in the clutch and allowed the engine to increase the speed gently.

He thought they would not need to divert to Flamanville. The wind was beginning to gust a little more and was settling and steadying. He anticipated a squall rather than a storm. Off a lee shore, he altered their heading to a more westerly track to ensure they had enough sea room to weather the squall and avoid stranding on the French coast.

The sky darkened rapidly. The wind started to change direction fluking and gusting. Abby went below and made a flask of soup and sandwiches. She reappeared stacking her efforts in the rack just within the door, then with two cups of coffee clutched in her hand she climbed into the pitching cockpit and settled next to Donny, passing his cup over and hooking herself onto the safety rail surrounding the open area.

The windscreen provided little real protection from the elements. Their foul weather gear was waterproof but the wet seemed able to penetrate anyway. The boat was now scudding along, much steadier in the water, as the wind increased and settled into a generally south-easterly direction. Their track would take them well clear of any hazards in terms of rocks or reefs, but the log indicated that their speed, even under reduced sail, was approaching nine knots. Donny had taken the engine out of gear, but kept it going. The running lights were all lit and the repeater screen for the radar indicated no contacts within its five mile radius. He leaned forward and switched to the ten mile range. Immediately two contacts showed up, the first astern about eight miles. The other towards the French Coast a smaller contact, probably a fishing boat, perhaps six miles to leeward.

That worried Donny in this wind. As he looked he felt the wind veer, suddenly turning fluky and boxing the compass before settling in a south-easterly to easterly direction, driving them towards the French Coast.

The contact astern was approaching steadily reducing the gap between them regardless of the weather. Donny was uneasy about this contact, without knowing why. He shrugged, thought about telling Abby about his instincts but was almost immediately distracted by the radio which burst into life. "Mayday. Mayday. This is *Guernsey Boy,* Prawner. I have lost my engine and I'm taking in water." The caller gave his position then repeated the message. The Coast guard in Jersey responded advising that their helicopter was already out. It could not respond for over one hour. They said that they had passed the request to the French but conditions prevented the mainland helicopter from operating. The life boat from Granville had been launched and would be with them in perhaps two to three hours.

The fisherman replied "The water is gaining on us. We may have to take to the life rafts.

Donny had looked at Abby and turned the *Swallow* in the direction of the position given, noticing that it was the smaller contact on the radar. With the wind behind them and the engine now running full out with the clutch in, the ketch was logging twelve knots. Donny picked up the mike. "*Guernsey Boy. Guernsey Boy.* This is British ketch *Swallow* approximately five miles west of your position. I should be with you within forty, four zero minutes to offer assistance. Over."

"*Swallow. Swallow.* This is *Guernsey Boy* your message gratefully received. I'll put the kettle on. Over."

Donny shifted in his seat and indicated for Abby to take over the steering. "I'll get things ready for whatever we can do. First he turned to the stern davit. He made sure the quick release was free and clear. This allowed the davit to swivel over the stern and drop the tender into the water, keeping the boat captive but available for immediate use. He then worked his way forward to the foredeck and hauled up the heavy rope and the sea anchor in case it was needed, lashing them ready to hand, on the pitching foredeck.

Back in the cockpit once more, he pulled out the flask and poured out soup for Abby and himself. Then concentrated on getting as much speed out of the boat as he could. He kept watch on the contact on the radar as it gradually came nearer.

Abby's voice called out. "Donny, come here and look. That's no fishing boat." She was pointing ahead. Dimly seen through the curtain of falling rain and flying spume was a big power boat, making bad weather of things.

Donny swung the wheel of the ketch turning away from the boat. They clawed back into the wind, with the engine flat out.

"It's seen us," Abby called. "It's turning towards us."

"Good luck to it." Donny called back. He switched on the radio and called the coastguard.

He asked them to confirm the identity of the so-called fishing boat in distress.

The reply came back. "No record of *Guernsey Boy* registered as a fishing boat, I suggest the call was a hoax."

"They are currently trying to follow me in what looks like a 60 foot motor cruiser. It is making heavy weather of it. I think they are in difficulties but I am not willing, or able to help. I am feeling threatened and am making off southward as fast as I can."

The coastguard acknowledged and wished them luck, reminding them that the whole conversation had been recorded. The helicopter would be with them within 30 minutes.

"That did it." Abby called. "They're turning away. Look!" she screamed. "It's gone too far round it will turn over." As she spoke the Motor cruiser was caught on the Port bow by a wave. The wind from the other direction forced the stern of the boat over, assisted by the rudder, hard over in the opposite direction. The wave won and the boat disappeared from view in a storm of spray and spume.

"It's gone." Abby cried. "Just disappeared out of sight. Do you think it has been sunk?"

"I doubt it," Donny answered. It looked a pretty well-found boat to me, they may have lost engine power but I doubt if it sank. Anyway there is no way I can help, even if I wanted to. They lied about the mayday. So it's their own fault."

For the next several hours they fought the elements, gradually hauling off from the French Coast and making south, to be ready to enter Granville when the weather front passed.

* * *

As forecast the weather eased by nightfall and they were able to enter the harbor. By nine they were moored alongside the visiting berth with the power and water supply plugged in. While Donny cleared things with the Harbormaster, Abby was able to enjoy the luxury of a long shower unworried by the amount of water she used.

Mr. Weston had been delayed in the Channel Isles. He was now due to arrive the following day, so the two youngsters were able to enjoy pizza and visit the local disco, without the sarcastic comments, they would expect from their respective parents.

Chapter Four

They met the ferry and collected Donny's father, then hustled him back to the boat. Over coffee they told him the entire series of events that had occurred over the past days since leaving Poole Harbor.

When they finished their story Weston looked at them both sitting opposite him in the cabin.

"Right. It is obvious to me that there is something on this boat that they want, whoever they are. The first thing to do is to search the boat from stem to stern and find it, whatever it is. Let's get on with it. Donny, hit the stern cabin. Abby, you've got the fore. I'll do here. Now get to it. I'm getting hungry."

They all dashed off to their allotted tasks.

* * *

It was only twenty minutes later that Donny found the package. It was taped to the bulkhead at the back of the double berth behind the pillows. "Peter could not recover the package while we were awake in the boat. But why did he try to kill us? If we had both dropped off to sleep he could have taken the package down and passed it on without the need to kill us.

The opened package lay on the cabin table: a pile of Euro notes, ten thousand in total and a small pile of papers covered in script. Finally the computer chip, actually a small memory stick. This, they had discovered, contained a schematic of some sort.

"Ah, food." Both Donny and his father called out together as Abby put the big bowl of stew on the table with lumps of coarse French country bread. With a ladle she served the stew out into bowls and they all set to as if they hadn't eaten for a month.

Afterwards they all sat back drinking wine and relaxing.

Abby got up in the end "Are we sailing today, or what?"

The men looked at each other and groaned as they got to their feet and went up on deck.

The sky was clear. There was no sign of the earlier bad weather. There were no ships in sight though there were three sails, all on the horizon. They had set course for Roscoff as Mr. Weston had arranged to meet an old army friend there. The trip was over one hundred and fifty kilometers so they expected to arrive by the following morning.

* * *

They reached Roscoff without further incident. With the boat moored alongside the pontoon the two youngsters wandered off to explore the town, leaving Mr. Weston and his friend Jonathon Glynn sitting in the cockpit of the *Swallow,* swapping lies and memories.

The couple wandered along the Quai de Charles de Gaulle. The busy waterfront was full of activity with summer-clad tourists mixing with local people dressed more soberly. The chatter of a variety of languages resonated in and out of the café's and shops.

They ate crab at a table on the pavement looking out over the Old Harbor with the boats lined up in elegant rows in the Marina and the odd boats, obviously local, moored out in the bay.

It took time for Donny to realize that they were being watched. It was with some chagrin that, when he mentioned it to Abby, she said, "I've know about it ever since we sat down here. I've been trying to find out where his friend is. I think I have him spotted now. Look over the road to the café opposite. Don't make it too obvious." The reprimand was in time to stop him swinging his head round to see the other watcher. As it was he did a half nod and left it at that.

"I presume they are the people who murdered Peter." Donny said thoughtfully. They are probably looking for the package we found in the *Swallow.*"

"And once they have the package, they won't need us alive anymore." Abby finished the thought.

"I think it's time we took the fight to the enemy. I'm getting fed up with looking over my shoulder all the time."

"Sounds good. How do we go about it?" Abby sounded positive enough but she was wondering how they could do something about a bunch of professional crooks who knew them. The only ones they knew were the two men following them at the moment.

"I think we have a word with dad's friend, Jonathon Glynn. He was in the army and then MI5 or 6 or something. He should know what to do. What do you think?"

"I'm afraid I can't think of anything at the moment. Possibly bang them over the head with something heavy. Otherwise I can't even begin to suggest anything."

"Well, we'll keep the head-bashing in mind in case we can't think of anything else. But first let's have a council of war with Dad and Jonathon."

He paid the bill. They left the Café walking hand in hand down the sunny waterfront back to the Marina.

* * *

The tall elegantly dressed figure leaning against the Louis XIV desk played with the lighter on the desk, idly spinning it round on its base, much to the irritation of the heavy-set man sitting behind the desk.

"For God's sake stop playing with the bloody thing and say something constructive. So far all you've managed to do is balls everything up. If I'd wanted that, I could have used Harry, here."

The stocky, battered man standing the other side of the room, showed nothing of the resentment that the remark caused. Harry Sanders had been around long enough, working with Meredith Jordon to know when to speak and when to keep his mouth shut. While the Boss gave the posh git, Marshall Smith, the benefit of his anger, Harry was happy to sit back and enjoy it.

Merry Jordon finished up. "You came to me with a foolproof idea. You said it was all sewn up, nothing to go wrong. That's exactly what has happened. It has all gone wrong. Your smart idea to use the kid's boat to get the gear out of the country worked all right. So why did you have to kill off the courier before you got the goods?

"Now get your arse off my desk and get things sorted out. I don't care how you do it as long as the gear is here on my desk, safe and sound with no loose ends by the weekend. I'll say no more. If it isn't....." Merry Jordon said no more. The unfinished sentence carried all the more menace because the meaning was plain.

The elegant Mr. Smith levered himself off the desk, shrugged his jacket so that it sat properly on his shoulders, sneered at Harry and left without a word.

"Keep an eye on things, Harry," the boss growled. "Slippery bastard is too cocky by half. If he fucks up this time, I'll not want to be seeing him again. Understand?"

"Got it in one, boss. I'll see to it." Harry went out of the door and strolled after the elegant suit to the door of the Chateau. He watched the departure of the white Ferrari, wincing slightly at the tearing of the tires as it took off at speed down the drive.

Harry kept things to himself most of the time these days. When he was much younger he had a habit of opening his mouth at the wrong moment. What he said was usually true, but he learned that telling the truth in itself was not always popular. After severe beatings on several occasions, it got through to him that there was a time and place for telling some truths to some people. Especially people who were in a position to hurt you physically. The lesson cost him a lot of pain, and lost him several friends. But it was a lesson well learned.

Looking after the departing Ferrari Harry decided that Marshall Smith had become a waste of space. Merry Jordan, the boss, would not be unhappy to see him gone. So provided there was no link to himself.....an accident of some sort perhaps, or even a bullet if the circumstances were right?

Harry strolled back into the house deep in thought.

* * *

While Harry was plotting his future, Mr. Marshall Smith was turning into the Imperial Hotel car park. He was cursing as he felt the chassis bottoming as he crossed the threshold of the downward-sloping access ramp.

Though the car was hired it still irritated him that he had to stay in places that were not really designed for the truly elite, or incidentally the cars driven by the said elite.

He hadn't always been involved with the sort of low class trash that he was forced to deal with in this day and age. In the past he had rubbed shoulders with the other gentry of his class. That was until his father had stupidly got hooked into Lloyds. Greed had dictated that he invest and guarantee more than the value of the entire estate in Devon, the town house in Mayfair, and the villa in Antibes. When the crash occurred the whole lot went, along with the substantial allowance that Marshall had regularly received. It had made things awkward to say the least, as the account had been overdrawn at the time. He admitted to himself now that it had always been overdrawn, but that didn't help.

He parked the Ferrari badly; taking up two bays, and walked away swiftly pressing the lock button on the key fob. He did not notice that the signal did not reach the car, and it was therefore still unlocked when Harry strolled down the ramp into the garage.

The small device looked harmless enough. It wasn't attached to the electrical system nor the exhaust. It was dropped into the driver's door pocket where it lay among the other bits and pieces that were the collected rubbish of the average driver. Harry strolled away having done what he came to do.

* * *

Marshall Smith seated himself in the lounge of the Imperial and ordered tea from the waiter. Then taking out his cell phone he made three swift calls, finally getting hold of the person he wanted. The message he sent was short and to the point.

"Lisette, the package is on the *Swallow,* a forty foot ketch in the Marina. There are two kids and a grown-up. They may or may not be aboard. They are all expendable. Just find the package and bring it to me. Do you need any help?" He listened for a moment to the reply. Then "Don't waste any time on this. I need a quick result." He shut off the call and sat back satisfied that the task would be carried out. He was not at all bothered by the fact that he had possibly condemned three people to death.

* * *

On the *Swallow,* the two young people had just returned. The four were sitting discussing the fact that Abby and Donny had been followed in the town. Jonathon had been inclined to dismiss their story as paranoia. Dan Weston quickly sorted the matter out before the fight started. "Jonathon, before you get sorted out by these two let me tell you that neither of them is likely to consider making a story like that up. Also as I told you earlier, Peter Davey was not mugged. He was deliberately murdered. My guess is, when he realized that the package was of importance, he tried blackmailing more money out of them. I think he was stubborn and wouldn't tell them where he had hidden the package. They got over enthusiastic trying to persuade him. He died without telling them where the package was hidden.

"Now they know we are here, they are keeping an eye on us and the boat, probably intending to ransack the boat when we are out. Alternatively, perhaps even when we are all here, they could kill all the birds in one stroke and search the boat at their leisure."

"In that case we should prepare to repel boarders." Jonathon said seriously. "I'll see what I can do about weapons." He rose to his feet, then stopped as he looked down the quay. "Oops. Looks like I'm a bit late." He indicated the figure of a woman flanked by two hefty men who were just turning onto the Marina pontoon. The three were peering at the names of the boats as they walked along.

Dan Weston looked at the woman and whistled quietly. "Wow. I must be in the wrong business. She is gorgeous."

Jonathon smiled grimly. "Don't be deceived, Dan. that woman is pure poison. To my knowledge she has killed at least three times and one of those involved the entire family of the victim: wife, three children and the nanny. We should get out of here, fast!"

Donny reached up and twisted the catch. As the locker opened he unclipped three automatics, and also one of the Armalites complete with magazine.

"Which would you prefer?"He asked Jonathon, who turned in surprise to be offered this selection of weapons. "Oh, uh. I'll have one of the Berettas." Jonathon said and took it from Donny and checked the magazine. Dan took another but he was still not sure that they would need them.

Jonathon made it quite clear that he had every reason to expect any action involving Lisette Delon would be swift and deadly if they were not prepared. "Be ready all of you." He looked round the group. Don't be deceived by her looks."

The men sat around the saloon and Abby slipped into the fore cabin to powder her nose, as she put it. She took the Armalite with her.

* * *

The French-accented English was sexy and friendly. "Excuse me, please, can I ask you for some help?"

Dan peered out of the doorway at the pretty face looking enquiringly at him. He took in the shapely figure, trim waist, long legs, and discreetly displayed bosom, and smiled back.

"Of course. Do come aboard." He glanced round, but could not see her two companions.

Holding his hand out he helped the lady aboard, ushering her into the cabin where Jonathon and Donny were seated.

Donny gulped as the short skirt rose up the woman's thigh as she stepped over the cabin sole into the saloon. Dan invited her to sit, and sat himself.

"I am Lisette Delon." She said in a flat voice, causing the three to look up in surprise. "You have something on this boat that I want. The easy way would be to give it to me. Her teeth bared and her mouth hardened. "The other way could be painful for you all."

For a long moment there was silence. Then "I have warned you! Now where is it?" With that she lifted her skirt showing a flash of blue lacy knickers.

Then the gun was in her hand covering the three men.

"So, who do I shoot first? Perhaps the boy?" She swung the gun towards Donny. The door to the fore cabin opened at that point. The Armalite fired with a thin crack. The pointing pistol dropped from the suddenly bloody hand. The bullet buried itself in the bulkhead. "Your friends are half way across the Marina now." Abby said "They were not happy facing this." She lifted the barrel of the Armalite still firmly aligned with the discreetly displayed bosom, which was now heaving a little with the emotion of the moment.

"Perhaps you ought to join them." Abby waved the rifle suggestively towards the door. Lisette got the message. She clutched her wounded hand, stepped onto the deck and from there onto the pontoon.

"This is not over." She said viciously. "I will settle up. You depend on it." She strode off down the pontoon wrapping her scarf around the bleeding wound.

As soon as Lisette had gone Abby collapsed onto one of the seats. Setting the safety catch on the Armalite she put it down at her side. "Wow. How about that then? She was something, wasn't she?"

The three males were still recovering. Donny said "She would have shot me. I'm right aren't I?

That bloody woman would have just shot me off-hand!"

"Well, she didn't. Thanks to Abby." Jonathon said seriously. "I'm sorry, Dan. I know the woman's record. I was caught on the hop as much as you two."

"You were right, Jonathon. That woman is stunning and has no qualms about using the fact. The blue knickers were distracting enough to allow her to draw her gun, before anyone could react."

The cool voice of Abby interrupted Dan's comments. "Correction, gentlemen. The blue knickers were distracting to you three. To me, it was obviously to cover drawing a weapon. So I was ready. Besides only a tramp would wear knickers like that under a mini skirt."

Donny stepped over to her. She collapsed against him. "God, I shot her. Just like that. I shot her. I thought she was going to shoot you." She was weeping now and Donny had his arms round her comforting her. Jonathon looked at Dan and said, "You are a lucky man to have youngsters like these two with you. You don't need my help when they are around."

Dan smiled wryly. "I had no idea, believe me. I am as impressed as you are. I'm proud of them both." While he was speaking he stepped across and wrapped his arms round the two youngsters in big bear hug.

Chapter Five

The *Swallow* rose to the gentle swell that had started building in the south Atlantic. As they passed Quimper and headed south there was only an undulating plain of azure blue. The wind riffles that drew the occasional white cap on the wide blue surface caused the occasional flutter to the luff of the mainsail. At the wheel Abby sat with her feet up, her bottom on cushion against the hard wood of the bench beneath. Her legs bared to the sunshine were bronzed and the bikini she was wearing revealed that the rest of her toned body had a similar color. With her sunglasses and the bleached streaks in her hair she looked every inch the sort of decorative crew member to be found on the leisure craft all over the Mediterranean.

The voices of Donny and his father, Dan, drifted up through the open cabin hatch as they discussed their plans for the mooring of the boat in La Rochelle. With two days still to go there was plenty of time to plan matters. The conversation was basically to cover the fact that both were anxious about the outcome of Jonathon Glynn's decoding efforts with the computer chip.

Persuaded that there was important information to be found on the chip, Jonathan had sent it to M16 Headquarters to give their code breakers the task of interpreting whatever could be found there. They had made the handover obvious and public. By this means Jonathan expected the attackers to leave the Westons and Abby alone.

The peace of the day was interrupted by the squawk of the satellite phone. Dan picked it up and answered the call. He spoke briefly to the caller listened then switched the phone off.

"That was Jonathon. We still have a problem from the sound of it. The opposition has been spotted getting on the train to La Rochelle. So it rather looks as though we are still in the firing line." Dan's face was grave as he contemplated the news. He started thinking of ways of eluding the possible pursuers.

Donny suggested they stop before they reached La Rochelle and leave the boat to be collected by the boatyard. They could depart by train back to UK or elsewhere even, leaving the villains stranded high and dry, waiting for a boat that never arrives.

* * *

Olonne-sur-Mer is in the Vendee Department, the starting point of the Vendee Globe race. Consequently the town is boat friendly and accustomed to the quirks and fads of the sailing community. There was no problem finding a friendly location for the *Swallow* to await collection by the yard in La Rochelle.

The group was en-route to Nantes by hire car within one hour of arriving in the port.

They passed through Nantes following the N137 stopping briefly for a snack before continuing to Rennes and St. Malo, to the ferry terminal.

Having dropped the car off, they were soon onto the ferry to Weymouth with their feet up, relieved that they had left their problems behind. "We should be able to collect the boat again when Ma is through with her meetings." Donny swung round to Abby; "You will be with us, won't you?"

"If I'm still welcome, I would love to come." She looked at Dan Weston who grinned at her.

"You must be joking. I thought you were part of the family." Abby blushed and didn't know whether to laugh or cry. With the tensions of the past week she had felt so much part of the Weston clan that it was almost a shock to remember that at home her mother would still be fussing about, making a show of bothering where she was. In fact, not really too concerned as long as she didn't interfere with the even tenor of her social life.

Abby felt guilty for that thought. Her mother really did worry about her, but Abby had taken over her own life ever since she reached the age of twelve. So her mother did not feel she needed to worry too much about what she did.

Mr. Weston had been quite honest with his comments to Abby, which had highlighted his attitude to her. The events of the past weeks had made her position clear as far as he was concerned. He treated her accordingly.

The passage across the channel eventually ended with their arrival in Weymouth. Mrs. Weston had driven down to meet them in the Land Rover Discovery. On the way home the conversation was deliberately light hearted avoiding the subject of the past few days.

* * *

It was nearly two weeks later when the two youngsters took the flight from Southampton. Jonathon had arranged to meet them at the airport and see them to the *Swallow* which was now in the water at the boatyard in La Rochelle. He would stay with them until Dan and Mrs. Weston arrived in two days time. Both had left their sailing gear on board so they were able to travel with carry-on bags only. This meant they had no need to hang about at the airport collecting luggage.

It all worked out well and when Jonathon greeted them, they were able to go straight off to enjoy a swim from the beach before they went to the boat.

Jonathon confirmed that there was no sign of watchers at the marina. So the two young people relaxed and spent the next two days shopping and wandering around the immediate area.

On the second day of their stay Jonathon greeted their return from town with a message from Dan Weston that there was a strike of local air traffic controllers. The flights to La Rochelle were cancelled. So the Weston parents were flying to Bordeaux instead. They should bring the boat down to Bordeaux to meet them by Saturday, in three days time.

Jonathon was apologetic. "I'm afraid I won't be able to come with you. Will you two be okay on your own?"

Donny grinned. "With all due respect, Jonathon, it's the James Bond stuff we're not so good at. Sailing we can manage."

Jonathon sighed. "Oh, youth, youth. Is there nothing you cannot do?" He answered his own question. "Do give me credit for something please. I was concerned about the James Bond thing, not the sailing. I know that to you I appear ancient, but age has some benefits. I am not by any means certain that the matter of the microchip has been disposed of, My instincts tell me that they will not have given up."

"You think there will be another attack when we go by sea?" Abby put in.

"That's just it. I don't know. What I do know is that I don't want to leave you in the lurch, out on the ocean with nowhere to run." The worry was apparent in Jonathon's voice.

"So it seems we will have to keep our weapons close and our trigger fingers poised." Abby said lightly. She struck what she thought was a John Wayne pose, with her right hand poised over her hip.

All three burst out laughing at this. Jonathon soon stopped and pointed out that there was more than a little truth in the comment.

* * *

In the sunshine the waters of the Bay of Biscay were as far from their evil reputation as they could be. The *Swallow* was scudding along under full sail with the Genoa set. Logging a steady 12 knots her crew estimated their arrival at Bordeaux, late afternoon on Friday.

At the helm Abby sat reveling in the sunshine with the breeze lifting her hair. They were surrounded by an almost empty seascape, the long line of the French coast low on the eastern horizon. A tanker was visible on the western horizon, the long smear of her funnel smoke painting the sky. The topsails of what appeared to be a schooner was making passage northwards slowly disappearing astern. A bowl of steaming stew appeared followed by Donny, dressed in shorts, who produced two spoons and a baguette.

He sat beside Abby and handed her a spoon and half the baguette, switching on the self-steering to allow her use both hands to eat. The boat adjusted its course slightly and the pair relaxed and shared the stew between them.

"We're making good progress. With this breeze we'll be in Bordeaux well before dark."

Abby was a little sad at the prospect of losing their privacy. They had said goodbye to Jonathon yesterday evening and they had been able to relax completely in each other's company, without feeling anyone was looking over their shoulder all the time. Although in fairness Jonathon had tried not to intrude on their privacy in any way, the mere fact that he had been present on the boat was enough to inhibit them.

* * *

Arriving in Bordeaux that evening they moored the boat and tidied up ready for the arrival of Donny's parents. That last night of their freedom was spent wandering the streets of Bordeaux hand in hand.

They had crepes from a roadside stall and wandered through the market as the evening turned to night, returning to the *Swallow* late to spend the night in each other's arms.

* * *

Dan Weston had elected to stay with the boat and provision it for the next stage of their trip; the stretch to Gibraltar and finally Malta, where the boat would be slipped and laid up for the winter prepared for next years' cruise in the Mediterranean.

The others had decided to take a two-day tour down to Biarritz, Donny, Abby and Mrs. Weston had hired a car and departed, leaving Dan Weston to do the hard work.

The hire car soared through the wine country of the southern Bordeaux region north of the Pyrenees. Donny, who had obtained his license on his seventeenth birthday, had been driving for some months now and handling the Seat version of the VW Polo was well within his capabilities, Abby sat beside him with his mother in the back. The trio had stopped in St Jean-de-Luz overnight and tasted the wine at one of the many vineyards in the region. The mixed case of white and red wines was tucked into the boot alongside the smoked ham and a collection of local cheeses, extra luxuries for the stores to be used on the trip to Gibraltar.

It was early evening when they arrived back at the boat they found Dan still sorting the stores he had ordered. Leaving the sorting until later, they all went out to one of the many small restaurants fronting the harbor to eat.

It was Abby who noticed that they were being studied discreetly by the people at another table in the dining room. She had accompanied Mrs. Weston to the ladies room and was following her back to their table when she dropped her hankie. She stooped to pick it up. As she rose to her feet once more she noticed the two men staring directly at Donny and Dan, who were both on their feet to receive and seat the two women back at the table.

It was not the looking she noticed particularly. It was the body language of the pair that struck a false note. She said nothing at first but as she returned to the table she decided to keep an eye on them. Seated she took her mirror out to check her make-up and used it to look at the men. One had a telephone to his ear and was looking at the party. He was speaking forcibly to whoever was on the other end. The other man was saying something but was being ignored by the man on the phone.

Not wishing to alarm Mrs. Weston she leaned over and whispered in Donny's ear what she suspected. Donny was seated in a position to see the table occupied by the two men. He was able to see that they were accompanied by two elegant women.

The two men made no overt move toward the youngsters. Perhaps the presence of the adults at the table deterred them. It was of course not certain that they were in fact the enemy, as Donny put it. Abby was convinced and made sure that they were not followed when they returned to the boat.

Dan discovered one reason why they didn't need to follow physically. Under the folding boarding platform at the stern of the boat he found a small radio beacon attached. They considered things for a while before deciding to re-site the beacon on a boat sailing to the Channel Islands. They managed things as the boat ran close, passing through the entrance to the harbor. They waved and chatted to the other boat as they both set out, started to leave at the same time. They made it a race of it, and were side by side passing through the narrows.

They were out of direct sight of the quay when the two boats separated amid gales of laughter and went their separate ways.

* * *

The comparative ease of the sail to Bordeaux had been deceptive. It did give the holidaymakers a sense of security that they would have been better without.

The discovery of the followers and the radio beacon had brought them back to earth with a bang.

The voyage to Gibraltar was a much more serious affair. Dan Weston talked to Donny and Abby about trying to do something about it.

He had been in touch with Jonathon Glynn on the subject of the memory stick. Though Jonathon could not elaborate on the content, it seemed that the information contained within the files was highly classified. They should never have been out of the hands of the Government Department from which they had been stolen.

Donny suggested that if they encountered their stalkers again, they should try and catch them to point out they were wasting their time.

Abby commented "They must know that the stick has been returned to the Lab, or whatever Department is involved. So chasing us has to be a matter of prestige, face, or something like it."

Dan nodded. "I'm afraid you're right, Abby. Since they have been on our tail this long I think we will have to discourage them once and for all. Let me think about it. Meanwhile, both of you consider ways we can use to get rid of our followers."

* * *

Marsden-Smith collected Lisette Delon and immediately said, "Well? What happened?"

Lisette touched her bandaged hand and said viciously. "You said nothing about them being armed, or that the girl is a bitch who can shoot like Annie Oakley. I got nothing except this." She held up her bandaged hand for him to see. She was furious, as was he, at yet another failure. He opened his mouth to shout at her. Before he could say a word, the device in the car door pocket exploded. It was small, very small, but the car was moving as usual at high speed along a country road. Marsden-Smith died immediately as the minute explosive shattered his left side, sending broken ribs through his heart and lungs. His grip on the wheel of the car relaxed and the camber of the road began to pull the car to the right. Before Lisette could scream, (she was still trying to take in the death of her companion) the right front wheel hit the curb on the long left-hand bend. This caused the sports car to flip high into the air, still moving at 140 kilometers an hour. Upside down, it smashed into the rustic stone wall that edged the vineyard beside the road. Both of the passengers took the full impact with the wall with upper part of their bodies.

* * *

When Harry Saunders heard the news he smiled privately. He reported to the boss that the British 'Git', as he insisted on calling him, had failed once more for the last time, and by the way, the Italian/French bitch Lisette Delon had shared his last moments.

Merry Jordan did like a nice clean slate. Now all they needed was to deal with the nosey kids and their parents. He was resigned to losing the memory stick. He would just make them pay instead.

Chapter Six

Donny and Abby were sitting on the float resting from their swim. Abby lay back and sighed. "I could get really used to this life. What do you say we drop off the map and beachcomb for the next twenty years?"

Donny grinned "In your dreams, babe, in your dreams. What would we live on?"

"On 'lurve' of course, like all the best romantic novels. What else?" Abby looked at him under lowered eyebrows, fluttering her eyelashes at the same time while deliberately slurring the word love.

Donny looked at her thinking to himself how lucky he was to have someone like Abby sharing his life. However long their relationship lasted he knew he never wanted to lose her. Abby had not mentioned it since Cherbourg, but he thought she still felt the same way. Correction, he hoped she still felt the same way. He shook his head. He was supposed to be thinking about ways and means of stopping the attempts of the ungodly to harm them. He shivered and looked around rapidly.

Abby giggled. "Okay, Hawkeye. Have you woken up again? I have been lying here unattended for at least five minutes while you disappeared into yourself. I hope you're back for good now. Otherwise I shall be forced to dump you in the ocean just to keep you awake."

With this remark she rose to her feet and leapt into the sea raising a shower of water that splattered over Donny in a satisfying dollop, causing him to jump up and follow her into the water.

Across the Harbor at Gibraltar there were three people sitting round a table with tall frosted glasses in front of them. Concealed by the central umbrella was a telescope through which they were observing the two youngsters playing around the raft. Despite the relocation of the bug placed on the northern bound boat, from information gathered from the conversations overheard, the watchers discovered the destination of *Swallow* was the Med. They had gambled that the logical place for them to call at would be Gibraltar. Harry Sanders had joined Albert and Felicia there as soon as confirmation came through.

"That's a good place to do them both." The voice was gravelly and the face was brutish.

"The girl is tasty." This one was a thin-faced young man with a face disfigured by the scatter of acne scars.

"You disgusting little oik." The woman had no time for the young man, who had leered at her when he was introduced for the first time. He had then suggested they went to bed immediately so that she would know that there was no point looking further for a lover. He had in fact established his credentials from the off. She decided that when she killed him she would make sure he knew just how much she appreciated his gauche advances.

The two men had come here from London while Felicia was based in Paris. She had moved from Kensington to be with her partner Harry Sanders. Of course, Harry spent a lot of time travelling. His new boss Merry Jordon was a restless man. He had interests in many different areas in UK and the EU. Luckily Harry reckoned he would be free before too long. He had decided that Merry had pissed him off once too often. After this job it would be all over and he would retire.

Felicia turned as Harry joined them at the table. "Seen enough?" he asked the group.

All three nodded in turn. "Right. I want suggestions from you all by tomorrow. They will be leaving in two days. The next opportunity won't come until they reach their next port."

"I do not intend to allow that sort of delay. I have plans." He looked at Felicia and winked.

Albert, the acne-scarred man said "I have a good idea for dealing with the girl." He leered at the group. The others turned away in disgust but Albert was quite unabashed. The smile on his face promised someone a bad time.

What the others didn't realize was that Albert was really way ahead of them when it came to brains and ingenuity. He had made up his mind to enjoy using the girl, Abby, before he killed her. He had practice. There were three unsolved murders in UK that he had carried out without being caught. This was a pretty straightforward job that he could enjoy. He would deal with the girl whilst they looked after the boy.

The meeting broke up a few minutes later. Back in his room Albert planned how he could get Abby alone.

The *Swallow* had been moored alongside the high quay. Even at high tide the mainmast stood just a few feet above the ground level. This did allow work to be carried out which would have otherwise required climbing the mast from deck level. By heeling the boat over, the mast head could be pulled over the edge of the quay wall, and the masthead lights could be serviced using a small collapsible scaffold.

Though this was convenient and safe, the two youngsters enjoyed the challenge of climbing the mast, albeit hooked on to safety lines. During the passages they had made both had become adept at the task even in rough seas.

The work done, the boat had been provisioned and moved out to a mooring buoy to free the quay berth for another boat. While they were at the mooring Dan Weston and his wife Mary were seeing some friends prior to their departure for Malta.

The foresail was unrolled from its reefed state to allow it to dry thoroughly. Abby lay on the deck in the shade just playing at reading a magazine. Donny was at the masthead hidden by the sail.

Albert knew his chance would come. He was out in the harbor on a sea-scooter, playing around scoring circles in the blue water and watching the *Swallow*, gradually getting nearer and nearer. He spotted no one else on the boat. He had no fear of Donny, even if he did appear. He would take his chance. As the scooter drew up beside the boat Abby stirred and rolled over to see who it was.

Albert looped the painter round one of the cleats on the boat and hauled himself aboard.

"Who the hell are you?" Abby said calmly. "And who invited you on board?"

Albert was taken aback by the calm voice and the lack of the fear his appearance usually inspired. Then he leered and said, "I've come to look after you, darlin'. You and your boyfriend have upset the wrong man. I've come to see you both off." His grin made it quite clear what his first priority was.

Abby shivered. This could be nasty. This wasn't Roger Harris. This man looked seriously danger-ous. Suddenly she remembered that Donny was up the mast. Had he heard? Did this man know he was up there? She almost looked up to see, but stopped herself. Instead she rose up to her full height, stretching as she did, to give the intruder the full benefit of her trim bikini-clad figure.

Albert almost drooled in anticipation. This was going to be better than he had imagined. Feasting his eyes on the girl he moved forward to grab her. Then the boat lurched. As he staggered to keep his balance he heard a swishing noise. He was struck incredibly hard in the ribs by the deck shoes, followed by Donny's full weight. He felt his ribs crack and found himself flying through the air over the tethered scooter. Eventually he hit the water of the harbor, with his ribs screaming in agony at the fresh impact.

As the waters closed over him he was trying to take a breath to replace the air knocked out of him by Donny's attack.

Donny swung back narrowly missing the mast on the return swing and grabbed to the stays to stop his flight. The *Swallow* rolled in sympathy with the violence of his swing but soon settled back level once more.

Donny dropped the last meter to the deck. He was immediately grabbed and hugged by Abby. "What were you thinking of, you idiot? You could have killed yourself doing a stupid thing like that. Wow?" She was crying and laughing at the same time so he just hung on to her and rode out the storm.

"Are you all right?" He said eventually.

"Thanks to you, I am." Calm once more she looked him in the eyes. What passed between them, unspoken at that moment, was a confirmation of the bond established that first day they got together at school. Very carefully and tenderly, she kissed him.

Unnoticed, the carelessly tied painter of the scooter slipped off the cleat and the little runabout drifted off.

Donny unshackled himself from the safety line, and took off his harness. The pair dived into the sea and cooled off. Neither even thought about the unfortunate Albert, who had not surfaced after his plunge into the sea. Apart from telling the story to his parents when they returned, Albert became a bad memory to them both.

* * *

Harry Saunders was not pleased. As he commented to Felicia later "The stupid idiot has buggered everything up as far as Gibraltar is concerned. It's good riddance. I'll choose my own crew in future."

Felicia, dressed in her skimpiest nightie, looked at him seriously. "Are you coming to bed, or what?"

* * *

On the *Swallow* Dan Weston said, "He did what? Horrified he turned to Donny, who was trying to disappear into the seat cushion and out of sight. "You do know I'm not insured for that sort of thing, don't you?"

There was a sudden silence. Then the entire group burst out laughing as the meaning of his words got through. Donny felt a weight lift off his shoulders. He had really expected a telling off, big time, from his father.

Afterwards his father took him to one side. "I could not fault what you did nor the reasons you had for doing it. Just please try not to worry your mother too much. I'm proud of you, son. That took guts."

The matter of the disappearance of Albert hardly created a ripple as far as the authorities were concerned. When the unknown body eventually turned up, it was linked to the stolen Scooter, already recovered. The battered state of the body was attributed to contact with the rocks around the peninsular. The matter was closed.

Chapter Seven

The sea was kind for the next few days and the voyage to Malta an easy one so when the boat finally tied up in Valetta three days later, the travelers were feeling ready for a shore excursion. They had deliberately not stated a port of destination when they left Gibraltar. They anticipated a trouble-free day at least, before trouble caught up with them again. They dined and wined in one of the waterside fish restaurants before returning to the boat to plan the final part of this summer cruise. The decision to overwinter in Malta meant leaving the *Swallow* in the boatyard on Gozo.

They left Valetta with the tide in the early morning, watched and followed by a cabin cruiser that kept discretely in the distance, hanging back toward the horizon. The whole time during that final day the cruiser kept pace. As Dan pointed out in these days of radar; following a boat could be comparatively easy. But as he also pointed out it was easy to spot a following craft as well.

They kept weapons handy the whole voyage, just in case.

The cruiser moored in the harbor at Gozo, and the watchers observed the party from *Swallow,* boarding the Malta ferry with their luggage. Harry cursed. Turning to Felicia he said."That's it then for now. Stick a bug on the boat. See if you can arrange for someone to call when they come to pick the boat up."

Dan and Mrs.. Weston took the luggage with them in a taxi to the airport. Donny and Abby could not resist making the trip in one of the local buses, converted from a WW2 army vehicle. The speeding, gear-crunching journey, took them round blind corners with the horn blaring, and no apparent regard for pedestrians or other vehicles.

Donny noticed that he could actually see the passing road surface through a large hole in the floor. Wisely he decided to keep that information to himself.

* * *

It seemed that they had lost their shadows at least whilst they were back in England.

Life continued more or less as planned. For Donny, having reached the age of eighteen, the move to Brunel University was the next stage of his career. Though he was disappointed that Abby had chosen Oxford to do her English/Law degrees, they still managed to meet regularly and spend time together.

During the long vacation they were due to meet up with Dan and Mary Weston in Malta. They planned to cruise round the eastern Mediterranean.

Donny had filled out. His smooth-muscled body was still without any spare fat. He trained regularly in the gym and was a member of the University Basketball team. He also ran the 400 meters in the athletic squad.

Abby had also managed to fill out in the right directions. Her trim figure reflected her dedication to keeping fit. As Donny observed she had managed to stay feminine with it.

* * *

The trip was much anticipated by both of them. It was with keen anticipation they arrived in Valetta to join the *Swallow* in Valetta Harbor.

There was no one to meet them at the airport. Both found this strange as they had discussed it on the phone with Dan before they got their flight.

"I hope there's nothing wrong." Donny was more worried than he sounded.

Abby wasn't fooled. "Let's get down to the boat and find out what's happening. It'll be a mix-up of some sort that's all."

Donny nodded. "Yes, you're probably right." He called a taxi across and told the driver to take them to the Marina.

As they approached they were greeted by the sight of flashing blue lights from a collection of police cars gathered at the entrance to the Marina.

The driver stopped in the queue of vehicles held up by the Police. Donny started to get out. He noticed a trio of people who were more interested in the people arriving in cars and on foot than the events taking place in the Marina. Something about their wary attitude rang a warning bell. He turned to Abby "I don't like the look of this. Those three over there seem to be on the look-out for someone. I think it might be us. God knows what has happened in the Marina. I just pray that the folks are alright."

Abby looked at the group Donny mentioned, keeping out of their line of sight. "Oh god, Donny, I have a bad feeling about this. I think they must have found the *Swallow* and waited until your folks arrived. I still remember that ugly man from La Rochelle. I thought I caught a glimpse of him in Gib but I wasn't sure at the time. Seeing him here is too much of a coincidence. This is trouble. "

Donny said, "I am going to find out what is happening. I know it doesn't look good but I have to know. They won't try anything with all this lot around. I'll appear further down the queue. You can join me when the police let the taxi through." He looked at Abby, his face drawn with worry.

She nodded. "Right. I'll keep a low profile and join you as soon as possible." She took his hand and looked into his eyes. "Be careful, love. Don't take chances. I don't want to lose you."

He looked back at her and squeezed her hand. "I'll be careful. I love you." Then he was gone ducking down in the shelter of the taxi and then moving down the line of cars before standing up. He walked to the policeman standing at the entrance to the Marina.

In the car Abby saw the watcher start up at the sight of Donny walking down the line of cars.

She called Donny's cell phone. "Donny, they've spotted you."

"Okay." He replied. Then he was speaking to the policeman at the gate

"What is happening here?" he asked. "My parents are expecting us at our boat, the *Swallow.* They will be worried."

At the mention of the name, *Swallow,* the Policeman spoke into his personal radio. Then he motioned for Donny to accompany his colleague into the marina.

The boat was moored alongside one of the pontoons projecting into Valetta harbor. The group of officials was standing beside the ketch from which the lights were forming patterns in the dusk of approaching nightfall.

The Detective in charge turned to Donny. "Are you Donald Weston?"

Donny nodded.

"I can tell you that your parents will recover. Both have been seriously injured. It seems they were mugged as they returned to the boat. The attackers stabbed them both. Happily the security man saw and sounded the alarm. The muggers ran off. I apologize. We are not accustomed to this sort of crime here in Malta."

"Where are my parents now?"

"They are in the City Hospital under guard. The muggers will be imprisoned for a long time. We will make sure that they do not get the chance to finish what they started."

"What do you mean 'finish what they started'?" Donny asked, knowing the answer anyway.

"I have been a police officer for many years now. To me this was a deliberate attack. Nothing was stolen. The attackers meant to harm your parents. Can you suggest why?" The lean thin faced Detective looked keenly at Donny.

Donny said "Outside the gate there are three people watching everything and everyone arriving and leaving here. One at least was involved in a smuggling operation that we spoiled for them. They tried to attack us before, during our trip to Malta last year. We thought we had eluded them. Any attack they plan or make must be revenge. The smuggling operation was over long since. No one was actually caught but they lost something of real value."

They moved down onto the boat and were now in the main cabin. Donny saw his mother's handbag and his father's jacket lying on the settee/berth.

The attack had taken place on the pontoon. Thank the lord it had. If it had taken place on the boat they may both have been killed.

The Detective's assistant came in and reported quietly. "The three people have gone. They were noticed by others standing near. They left in a black Audi car, shortly after you arrived. If what you say is true, they probably waited to see that you were here, then left. Possibly to arrange something for your benefit."

There was a disturbance on the pontoon outside followed by the appearance of Abby carrying the two bags from the taxi. She promptly dropped the bags and threw her arms round Donny's neck and hugged him. "Oh, Donny. They told me. Your mum and dad both in Hospital, the swine!" There were tears in her eyes as she drew back to look at him.

The cough from the Detective interrupted the reunion. Abby stepped back. Donny introduced him to Abby.

"I will leave men here tonight to see you are not disturbed. You will probably want to visit your parents in hospital first. My car will take you and bring you back. Tomorrow you make your own arrangements. I would like to speak to you at the Police Headquarters sometime in the morning."

"Thank you very much for everything, sir. You have been most helpful. Thank you for saving my parents. We will go and see them now if you wouldn't mind."

* * *

Dan Weston was awake when they arrived at the hospital. He greeted the pair with a wan smile and considerable relief.

The policeman on duty went and sat outside the room, giving them time to talk privately together.

"Well, am I glad to see you both. Your mother was worried sick that they would get to you before we could warn you. They caught us as we were walking down to the boat after eating this evening. They came out from the shelter of the other boats on the pontoon. Three people, a woman and two men. The woman was as bad as the men. She cut my arm as I put it up to cover your mum. The men both jumped in. They all acted as if they were going to hurt us as much as possible before they killed us. It was lucky they did because they only had time for a couple of stabs before the security man started blowing his whistle. He came running after them with his gun out. The dark man said he would be back to finish the job sometime soon. Then they ran off the other way. The security man called the police and the ambulance. Then I fainted. Your mother roused me when the ambulance arrived."

There was a knock on the door. An orderly wheeled a gurney in with Mrs. Weston. She was gently placed in the second bed in the room. She was conscious. "Thank god you are alright. I was worried you would just walk into trouble, like your father and I."

Donny said, "We have to call on the Police tomorrow. We got a look at the three people who did this, and the police have a description. We'll keep our eyes open while we are in Malta." He reached behind his back and produced one of the pistols from the armory on the boat. "I promise we won't take chances. If they do try anything I won't hesitate to use this." Tucking the gun back in his waist band, he kissed his mother and shook his father's hand. Abby hugged them both and they left the hospital.

"We should eat before we return to the boat. I'm sure there will be plenty of food there. I don't fancy having to prepare it at this time of night. Is that okay?"

Abby nodded. "That's a good idea."She turned to the driver "Do you know somewhere where we can eat quietly?"

The driver grinned. "I know a nice place." He dropped them off at a restaurant, promising to pick them up as he had been instructed by Superintendant Jacobi, the officer in charge of the case.

Donny and Abby ate silently at first. Then, as the meal progressed, Abby said, "We are going to have to find these people. How dare they attack innocent people just like that. I for one refuse to hide myself away, just because they have some sort of grudge against us."

Donny smiled at her "Why am I not surprised to hear you say that? I would have been disappointed if you had reacted differently. Tonight we sleep. Tomorrow we look. Agreed?"

"Agreed." Abby took his hand across the table. "And the bitch is mine. Okay?"

Donny looked at her surprised. Then shrugged, "She's probably a handful." He left it at that and kept his reservations to himself.

They talked generally about the boat and what they would need to complete the provisioning. They had already decided that they would collect the parents from the hospital as soon as they could travel. They both felt they would be safer on the boat. It would allow them a free hand in acting against their opposition.

Over the next three days they walked the streets of Valetta, keeping a lookout for any of the three people who had attacked the Westons. They had no luck. Donny suggested that they had probably left the island already.

Mr. and Mrs. Weston came out the hospital on the third day and joined them on the boat. They sailed at lunchtime the same day. Neither Donny nor Abby told them what they had been doing. They merely said they had spent their time sightseeing.

Since neither parent had suffered life threatening injuries they had been released on the assurance that they would see a doctor and have their dressings changed within three days.

* * *

The voyage to Crete was a time they all needed to wind down and plan. The fair weather and light winds all conspired to relieve the tensions of the past few days. Once there, the wounded obeyed their instructions. The Cretan doctor was able to give them dressings to change for themselves in the future. Both were healing well and back on their feet.

It was while shopping in the market in Iraklion that Abby spotted the woman. She thought that maybe the woman had not seen her.

She put on a headscarf and sheltered behind a lace stall. With her big sunglasses she emerged in time to follow the woman through the streets to the Continental Hotel. When she entered Abby watched her walk over to the reception desk. She was given a key by the attendant, who openly watched her, admiring the sensuous sway of her bottom as she walked over to the bank of elevators. Abby said longingly. "I should have a figure like that." The receptionist turned and looked at her. Gallantly he said, "You have nothing to worry about, Miss. It has taken Madam Wagrim much training and dieting to achieve what nature has already blessed you with."

They both watched as Madam Wagrim entered the elevator which, she noticed, ascended to the third floor.

The receptionist said with a smile "Can I help you, Miss?"

Abby hurriedly replied. "Oh, I nearly forgot. My parents asked me to find out the cost of staying here. They intend coming later this year."

When the man handed over the brochure for the hotel she thanked him prettily. "You have been most helpful and diplomatic, sir." She gave him a big smile. As she left she swayed her bottom for his benefit.

Having arranged to meet Donny, she made her way to the Cathedral where he was waiting.

The news that the enemy had second-guessed them was not good. Donny muttered "I think we will have to do something about this."

Despite speaking under his breath, Abby heard him. "I agree" she said.

He looked up sharply. "You mean that?"

At her nod he said, "We cannot let the parents know. We will probably need to do something drastic, like kill them to stop them killing us."

Abby stared into his eyes. "I will not let them do what they did to your mother and father again. I have no doubts. I'll do whatever is necessary to see them safe. Remember the woman is my problem. Agreed?"

Despite his own misgivings Donny agreed. "Tonight, we'll go calling."

* * *

It was dark. The streets were busy at nine thirty that night. Having eaten on the boat with Dan and Mary, the youngsters had declared that they were going out dancing. They left, hand in hand, for the center of town.

There were people everywhere, milling about drinking and eating in the warm summer air.

From the hotel the woman appeared, accompanied by the two men who had been with her in Malta. As they picked up the trail, they noticed the man who appeared to be in charge of the group answering his cell phone. He stopped and spoke to the other two. The other man turned and stopped a cab. All three climbed in. The taxi turned in the street and started back to the hotel.

Donny and Abby turned round and walked the short distance back to the hotel. They watched while the leader dashed in and returned a few minutes later with a carry-on bag. The others had stayed in the waiting taxi.

Abby called a cab over as the returning man jumped into the waiting taxi. It took off with the two young people following it in another cab. They went straight out to the airport.

They watched the leader check in for a flight to Paris. He disappeared through the entrance at a run while the announcement of the departure of the Paris flight was being finally called.

The remaining man and the woman turned and left the airport building calling a cab once more to return to the city.

Abby and Donny followed.

The pair ate at a restaurant near the Cathedral in one of the quieter streets behind the massive building. It was difficult to get a good view of them whilst they ate so Donny and Abby waited in an alley opposite the restaurant for them to appear.

Chapter Eight

It was while they were still waiting that the voice behind them made them realize that they had been spotted. They had been tricked "Just come down the alley quietly." The gravelly voice of Madam Wagram's companion spoke from behind them. "This is not a toy. The gun he waved did not look like a toy to either of them.

The woman was waiting for them. "Well, well. How nice of you to make things so easy for us. Harry will be sorry he missed this. He does enjoy watching me take pretty girls apart." She looked at Donny. "I'm sure you'll enjoy this little exercise even less than your girlfriend here."

As she spoke she lashed out with her right hand at Abby's face. What happened next took them all, except Abby, by surprise.

From nowhere the hand was knocked aside. Abby's long left leg unhampered by the mini skirt she was wearing, rose sharply showing a flash of white lace. Her foot hit the woman's face with a thwack that made Donny's captor wince. The man stood open-mouthed, distracted, unused to seeing his partner opposed like that. In his moment of inattention Donny saw his chance and took it. The gun had moved and Donny's fist hit the man's wrist with a smack that caused the man to drop it. Donny's other hand was already drawing the Beretta from his waist band. As it came free the safety came off and the first bullet hit the thug in the stomach, causing him to double over to meet the next shot in his face. The man was dead before he hit the ground.

Donny swung round to the woman, but Abby called. "She's mine, remember." She evaded another punch from the woman and returned it with interest making the woman gasp as her blow struck her antagonist in the neck.

The two women circled each other. Then as Abby stepped forward the woman produced a knife. Her expression changed. Weaving the knife before her she caused Abby to step back. The alley surface was uneven. Abby stumbled as she retreated from the knife blade before her. The woman lunged forward, the knife at stomach level. Abby stopped. Her hand grasped the wrist of the hand holding the knife.

The two stood locked in the position straining to gain control of the knife. Abby's other hand stabbed forward hitting the woman in the ribs, causing the woman to gasp. Her greater strength seemed to be winning the battle for the knife. The blade crept up towards Abby's stomach.

Abby suddenly seemed to give way. The knife arm swung up. Abby's body was no longer in the path of the blade. It rose in an arc. Suddenly it was moving back toward the woman's chest. She slowed its progress. Then screamed as Abby relentlessly forced the blade into her attacker's body.

She applied pressure, her face set and determined. Finally she stepped back as the woman staggered, gazing unbelievingly at the hilt of the knife projecting from just below her left breast. She looked up at Abby, hating her with her eyes. Then she collapsed to the ground, her eyes glazing over dead.

Donny stood there, gun still in his hand, looking at Abby.

"Let's get out of here before someone comes." Abby said tensely.

Donny shook himself and bent down to go through the pockets of the dead man. He emptied everything out. Then he wiped the gun butt and placed it in the woman's hand. He then pulled the man nearer to the woman and placed his hand round the haft of the knife still lodged in the woman's body.

Then, gathering the man's gun—a Walther unlike his own—and his possessions, they left quietly by the other end of the alley. No one had seemed to notice the noise, or the altercation. Probably the noise of the street was sufficient to cover the subdued gunshots.

Abby checked her clothing as soon as it was light enough to see. Luckily there was no sign of blood on her clothes. They both made a bee line for the nearest pavement café where they sat down to recover from their brief ordeal.

The gun was concealed where his own had been kept, tucked into the rear of Donny's waist band. Now they were able to examine the contents of the pockets of the man they now knew to be named Rupert Dawson of Raynes Park, South London. There was a clutch of Euro notes and change. Plus several written notes on scraps of paper, a hotel key and an airline ticket for the end of the week. The small diary was full of neat writing. Donny put it away to study later.

They had a coffee and a brandy each. Then hand in hand started to walk back to the boat. After a few paces Donny lifted the room key-card, and said, "Hang on. Let's take a look at the blokes room." He turned to Abby. "Okay?"

"Why not? Let's do it." Abby felt a little light headed, reckless even, willing to go for it while they were at it.

The foyer of the hotel was busy when the strolled in. Abby, without her big glasses and head-scarf was relieved to see the receptionist had changed. The two wandered over to the bank of elevators and went up to the third floor. Donny dropped the room key into the card slot. They went in, quickly closing the door.

The room was tidy and the single case was lying closed on the second bed. Donny tried the wardrobe. It was not being used. He swept up the washing gear from the bathroom and put it in the bag provided. Then putting the bag in the suitcase he looked around the room. There was a communicating door to the next room. On impulse he tried it. It was open and was obviously the woman's room. Her clothes were scattered around the room. A briefcase was thrust partly under the bed. Abby pulled it out and checked. It was locked.

Her case was in the wardrobe so Abby gathered up everything and crammed the things into the suitcase. In the bathroom she did the same. Donny went out to the balcony overlooking the alley. He turned to Abby. "I'll go down and catch the cases when you throw them down. Then no one will see us carrying them through the lobby."

He turned back, went through the door into the hallway. Then went down the stairs to the lobby and out of the side door into the alley. As Abby dropped the two cases he caught them, then the briefcase.

To his surprise Abby climbed over the balcony rail and caught hold of the drainpipe. From there she descended to the ground.

"Come on. There are people going into the room next door." She said. Grabbing one of the cases, she left him with the other and the briefcase, and made off down the alley to the rear of the hotel.

They agreed that they would have to return to the boat with the cases. There was nowhere they could safely examine the contents without renting a room somewhere.

* * *

Back at the boat Dan was up sitting in the saloon with a drink in front of him. Mary was, according to him, sound asleep in their cabin.

He looked at the two suitcases and the brief case, as they bundled through the door. He said nothing until they were seated in turn, with drinks in front of them.

Donny looked at Abby. Dan spoke first "Whose are the cases?"

Donny elected to answer. "They belonged to two of the trio who were watching for us. Two of the people who, we are sure, stabbed you and Mum."

Dan thought for a moment. "Do I take it that they will not be needing them anymore?" His voice slowed down as the full impact of his own words got home to him.

Donny shrugged uncomfortably under the steady gaze of his father. "They tried to capture us. We were ready for them."

Dan leaned over and operated the catch of the armory. The door dropped revealing the space where one of the Berettas had been seated.

Wordlessly he held his hand out. Donny retrieved the weapon he had recovered from Rupert Dawson. It was a Walther PPK.

Donny shrugged. "I had to put our gun in the hands of the woman, and wrap his hand round the knife handle. At least then they could think they had killed each other."

Dan had hoped that he would never hear his son saying such things. He took the Walther and removed the magazine. Then taking out a pair of thin rubber gloves and the cleaning kit, stripped the gun and carefully cleaned the whole thing. He reassembled it placing it in the rack where the missing Beretta normally rested, then closed the door.

"Tell me." He said.

Between them the two told the story, starting with their reasons for looking for the trio of watchers in the first place.

Dan looked sharply at Abby when they came to the part where she had fought the woman. But he said nothing until their story was complete. Then he said "Well. There's nothing we can do about what has already happened. We should have a look through the cases and see what we can find. For what it's worth I agree that what you did was the right thing to do. Even though, I am sorry you did it by yourselves."

They then took the first of the cases and went through the contents piling the clothing on the table. There was nothing but clothes in the first case, all feminine. The other was neatly packed with men's clothing. Between the ironed shirts was a plastic folder. There were layers of banknotes in the folder amounting to several thousand Euros. There was also a twin to the Walther PPK with two spare magazines.

The briefcase locks succumbed to the talented fiddling by Dan with a paper clip. He took great care opening the case making sure there were no booby traps to trap the unwary. Satisfied he opened the lid revealing packs of money filling the body of the case. In the lid there were several folders containing histories of people including Dan and his wife and Donny and Abby. There was also a collection of documents, passports and driving licenses and credit cards in different names, all had the same photograph: the woman they knew as Felicia Wagram.

Dan recognized her as the woman who had attacked them.

Dan removed the money and the files from the briefcase, putting them together with the money from the other case.

Donny produced the things he had recovered from the dead man. Once again Dan recognized the man from his license photograph. The little notebook contained, written in neat writing, the details of the disposal of several people from a variety of places all over Europe.

Donny sighed with relief. His one fear had been if they had got the wrong man and woman.

Then they collected all the other things together and closed up the suitcases.

"We'll sail tomorrow and dispose of these cases at sea. Now, young lady. This fight you had with the woman. What was that all about?"

Abby blushed. Then, "After our first voyage together, when we had the problems with these people I felt quite helpless. I realized that, had we been attacked, I would have been useless.

"When I got to Uni I noticed that one of the societies was martial arts. So I joined. Over the past year I concentrated all my spare time in learning the discipline, basically Tai Kwan Do. As my Sensei said in modern times the martial arts overlap. The techniques are modified to deal with the specialist moves of companion disciplines. I have reached the Black Belt, I intend to continue next year to progress as far as I can within the time available."

Donny never found out what his father told his mother about that night. They sailed in the morning for Thita (Santorini) where they planned to stay for a few days at least.

* * *

Jonathon Glynn bumped into them there. A meeting that Donny confided to Abby was a bit too coincidental. Dan Weston obviously came to the same conclusion. He called the pair to the foredeck and quietly explained that the attack had been reported to Interpol as the name Weston had been put up for special attention throughout the European area after the attempted smuggling incident.

Apparently the Police in Crete had identified the two assailants. They had obviously fallen out and killed each other. The third member of the party, Harry Sanders, was believed to have escaped taking all their luggage with him. They had traced him to Paris but lost the trail at that point. He was described as British. From the security camera at the airport it was subsequently confirmed that both the dead were still alive when the Harry left Crete. The belongings of the two dead had been removed from their hotel rooms by person or persons unknown.

* * *

They managed to enjoy their holiday. The parents healed and were able to take more and more part in the physical side of things. Though it was obvious that the effect of the attack on Mary had been more traumatic than they had all at first assumed. She became generally more self-absorbed. Though she made an effort to join in to the activities of the others, it was obvious that her heart was not in it.

Abby mentioned it to Donny. "I am worried about your mother. The attack seems to have taken the heart out of her. Have you noticed anything?"

"I know Dad is worried about the same thing. He spoke to me about returning home early with her. He did not want to leave us in the lurch. I told him we would manage. After all we have plenty of money in the kitty after the last little exercise. I think he may take me up on the offer."

"Where are we leaving the boat at the end of summer? Nobody has mentioned it up to now."

"Bluntly, we had not decided. Dad discussed it with me before we came away. We decided to make our decision while we were here in the Med. I'm inclined to favor one of the UK ports, perhaps Cobh in Ireland. It's a long cruise but we have the time. I think it will be some time before the family does a summer cruise again. I thought, by keeping it within range but away from home, we would be able to use her ourselves without upsetting Mum by turning up and reminding her of this year's attack."

Abby put her arms round Donny's neck. "You are a thoughtful lad sometimes, Donny Weston. I love you for it." She kissed him on the lips. He held her close enjoying the feel of her body pressed firmly against his.

"And you, Abby Marshall, are going the right way to finish up in the fullness of time as the permanent half of a partnership already committed to by me."

He felt her tense momentarily. Then she relaxed and looked at him steadily. "Am I to take you seriously?" She asked.

"I was never more serious in all my life," he said matching her mood. "I thought perhaps when we qualify?"

"Let's keep that in mind and take things as they come."

Dan and Mary left the island by air the following day. Donny spoke to Jonathon as they watched the plane leave.

The small notebook retrieved from Rupert Dawson was handed over plus the passports and other documents from the woman's possessions. Jonathon had been told by Dan that the stuff had been taken from Rupert and Felicia's rooms with the rest of their luggage when the two were out accompanying Harry to the airport. So Jonathon accepted the items without question. He was happy to hear their plans for returning to the British Isles, albeit Eire. It would be far easier to keep a discreet eye on things in the future.

Thus it was that the two young people were able to depart from Santorini on the longest voyage of their lives. Happily minus the location bug, planted by Harry Sanders and removed by Jonathon who had placed it on the hull of an Orient bound motor cruiser. As he observed it would be interesting for the opposition to follow, since it was scheduled to call at several exotic ports on the way. He left the little bug detector with the boat just in case.

Chapter Nine

Lazy days sailing the length of the Mediterranean were an idyllic time for Donny and Abby.

Without the inhibition of having parents about they were able to be completely natural together. For long periods of the time they did not even bother to put any clothes on. Stopping now and then to swim and play in the warm waters and climbing out to lie on the deck and dry off in the warm sunlight allowed them to relax completely for once. They learned more about each other than either realized. The main lesson was that their relationship was based on a genuine liking for each other which, combined with their physical attraction, augured well for their future.

They made a diversion into the port of Tangier before the stretch up the coast of the Iberian Peninsula.

While they were anchored in the bay they were contacted by a colleague of Jonathon Glynn. Martin Smith was a young man with straw-colored hair and a surfer's tan. He hailed them from the deck of a passing cruiser, inviting them for a drink.

Donny looked across at Abby who nodded and they met an hour later in a waterside Bistro over a tray of ice cold drinks being shared around several young people holidaying in the city.

Martin eased them both to one side away from the noisy group and identified himself as a member of M16, known to Jonathon Glynn, who had suggested they might be found around here by today.

He then told them that the man who had gone to Paris, named Harry Sanders, was the partner of Felicia Wagram, the woman who died in Iraklion. Apparently Harry was a known man with a reputation for successful operations. He had been unable to complete his brief in Crete. It was considered that the outcome may have been different had he missed his flight and stayed that night. The main purpose of the message was that Harry now regarded the matter to be personal. He was anticipating dealing with it himself, so the two youngsters were in serious danger.

He, Martin, had been told to offer his services as extra protection for the remainder of their voyage home.

He was dragged off by one of the girls of the party at this point, leaving Donny and Abby alone.

"I don't like this. He is probably all right but I prefer not to trust our lives to someone like him." Abby said, with her lips pressed firmly together, as she watched Martin dancing around the floor with a girl on each arm.

"I agree with you." Donny took her arm and casually wandered off down the quay to the spot where they had parked their dinghy.

It was gone.

"Why am I not surprised?" Donny said and walked further down the quay to the point where local boatmen hired themselves out for tours and as a water taxi service.

He hired a small boat driven by an ancient Seagull outboard, and asked the driver to take them to their boat. On the way to look out for their dinghy that had come adrift from its place by the quay.

The smiling boatman grinned and said, "No problem, master. Your boat will be quickly found." He gunned the engine and they pottered out into the waters of the bay, the darkness patterned with the reflections from the electric lights of the City and the scatter of occupied boats at anchor across the water.

In minutes only, the drifting dinghy came into view bobbing gently in the waters with the painter hanging over the bow Abby's carefully tied knot, deliberately untied. There was no way that the knot had untied itself. They picked up the dinghy and went on to the spot where the *Swallow* lay. Donny boarded and made a quick recon through the boat to make sure there were no unpleasant surprises awaiting them. Then he asked the boatman if he had seen who had released their dinghy.

"Your friend, who went to the café with you, came out and sat out beside the edge of the quay. I think he was having a joke on you, perhaps?"

"Perhaps he was." Donny replied. He paid the boatman and Abby went up to the bow and hauled in the mooring rope.

She called out quietly to Donny, and stopped bringing in the line. Standing leaning on the pulpit she pointed mutely at the water below. The shadowy outline of the body was looped onto the bow rope. Donny hauled the dead man to the surface. He looked English, clean shaven dressed in shirt and shorts. With difficulty they hauled the corpse onto the deck. Donny checked the pockets. In the man's hip pocket he found a crunched up hotel booking confirmation, addressed to Martin Smith.

Donny looked at Abby. "Why do I think we were being had?" He asked. "That Martin Smith ashore never gave me any confidence. I think it's time we sailed, don't you?"

They released the buoy and Abby loosed the foresail allowing it to draw the boat's head round to the open sea. Donny hauled the Mainsail up and stepped back to the cockpit to release the Mizzen. He set the self-steering while Abby and he set the sails to get the boat steadied on course for the open Atlantic. Off to the north the towering bulk of Gibraltar moved astern as they progressed rapidly with the freshening wind into the ocean swell.

Once they were well out to sea and completely out of sight of the lights of Tangier, they took a photograph of the body and then consigned it to the depths with two pieces of the ballast attached to his ankles. Abby said a prayer for him. Donny decided that if he saw the pseudo Martin Smith he would probably shoot him.

Well clear of the land they stood north for two days steering to clear Cape St Vincent. The light gradually shifting from north-east to due east before dropping out of sight as the second night passed. They stood watch and watch for the first forty-eight hours, before finally settling back into their normal routine.

They discussed the death of Martin Smith and came to the conclusion that they were going to be forced to remove the threat posed by Harry and his friends. They agreed at that time to take their next year out. Since both had completed their first year at University, and both now knew they were through the end of term exams successfully, taking a year out was possible. The pair decided at that point that the hunt for the person or persons responsible for the attack on Donny's parents and the murder of Martin Smith was on.

Abby pointed out that the killer of Smith had been out to the *Swallow*. "It's possible that they have installed another of their location bugs. I think we're going to have to do another complete search of the boat just in case."

Donny thought for a moment. "I wonder if Jonathon's bug detector still works?" He leaned across the cabin and popped the catch on the armory. The panel dropped and he lifted a corner of the foam disclosing the small leather case that housed the electronic scanner.

"While I check this out, perhaps you could check the guns. See that they are loaded and ready for action, just in case."

As Abby set to, he opened the case and removed the small electronic device. He switched it on and the red light lit immediately. It also started to flash and issue a faint beeping noise. As Donny swung round the beeping and flashing increased then decreased in frequency. Steadying the noise at its loudest he moved in the direction indicated coming to a point on the bulkhead where there was nothing at all, no blemish, nothing to indicate any interference at all. Puzzled he stopped and looked at the device. All seemed in order, then he blinked and reached round the bulkhead through the door and ran his hand behind the clock mounted there. His fingertips touched something behind the clock. When he probed with the blade with his knife he caused a small disc to fall to the deck. He picked it up and stepped out to the cockpit and dropped it over the side. Then starting from the stern her systematically swept the boat from stern to stem.

There were three more bugs found during the meticulous search. All went into the sea. As the final bug dropped Donny heard the whup, whup, whup, the sound of the blades of a helicopter approaching.

He called to Abby. "Get the Armalite and an H&K out. There's trouble coming." He scrambled down into the cockpit and took the sub-machine gun from Abby. She had the Armalite in her other hand. Having passed over the smg, she picked up the spare magazine for the Armalite, slotted in its place and loaded the first round.

The helicopter was a standard Bell Longranger helicopter that dropped down to sea level as it approached. Donny suddenly realized they were checking on the name painted on the canvas dodger either side of the cockpit. The machine rose, the occupants satisfied they had the correct boat and the first stream of bullets shattered the sea on the port side.

The helicopter was too far away from them to use the H&K. But from behind his head he heard the crack of the Armalite. The Bell jerked but flew on, obviously not badly damaged. It swung round across the boat to the starboard side. As it flew past Donny chanced a burst from the smg, but without apparent effect. As the Bell turned to run parallel along the side of the boat the Armalite fired again. This time the bullet hole in the canopy was visible. The Helicopter turned away. Immediately both

Donny and Abby started firing at the tail spinner. This time there was a noticeable result as the Bell staggered. The people in it realized how vulnerable they were without the ability to stand off and attack out of range of the guns on the boat below. The helicopter went into a circle around the boat keeping its distance. Donny focused his binoculars on the Bell. He recognized the face of the man who had introduced himself as Martin in Tangier. He called the news out to Abbey. She had been shooting from the open port either side of the cabin. Now she came into the cockpit. "That's better. Now I can see properly."

She watched the circling Bell for a few moments then she wrapped the sling of the rifle round her forearm, leaned against the heel of the boat and let her breath out slowly and fired, one, two, three, four, five, six times.

Donny watching through binoculars saw the holes appear in the canopy silently. For a moment nothing happened. Then there was a twitch and the Bell seemed to stop in mid-air. It dropped like a stone. The door opened and a man appeared. Abby fired once more. The man fell back into the machine which hit the water with a huge splash, the rotor slapping the sea into brief frenzy. There was a panicky attempt to open the door of the helicopter. The shock or perhaps the gunfire had warped the door. The struggling figure could not get the door open. The whole machine sank out of sight before the ketch had a chance to get near the spot.

The waters were smooth and unbroken by the time they sailed over the site of the crash. Neither of the two youngsters felt particularly proud of their achievement in bringing the Bell down. But as Donny said at the time, "They made it quite clear that they were here to sink us. Out here in the open sea killing us was going to be their kindest act. I would have picked up any survivors but I would not have guaranteed that they would have made it to land."

Abby was silent for a while. Then "We had already decided that we would take the war to them. That was the first skirmish as far as I'm concerned. I think we won that one. I hope and pray we keep winning because I want to live my life without looking over my shoulder for the next twenty years."

She turned to Donny and put her arms round his neck. They hugged each other, happy to be still alive.

* * *

For the rest of the voyage home they had the chance to practice with their guns. Within the confines of the cabin Abby showed Donny some simple moves that could be useful in a tight corner. The fact was that these encounters more often resulted in them collapsing with laughter and occasionally in each other's arms sharing the joy of lovemaking in the dip and sway of the boat in the Atlantic swell.

Their return to home after placing the boat at Cobh in Eire was a low-key affair. They confided to only Dan the events that had occurred on the journey home.

Not surprisingly Dan was very upset on hearing about the attempt to kill them when they were attacked by the helicopter party. He was especially worried about the murder of Martin Smith. He managed to get hold of Jonathon Glynn, who came down to Ringwood to discuss matters with Dan, Donny and Abby.

"I'm especially concerned about the fact that they have continued to try to eliminate the pair of you. It is out of character for the average crime boss to be so persistent. The loss of the helicopter must have cost him dear, aside from the men involved. As I understand it, this business has cost the lives of seven people, including our man Martin Smith and your Peter Davey. This whole scenario is becoming more like a vendetta every day. You are all in danger now. From my point of view you should all be placed under 24-hour protection."

Donny held up his hand at that point. "That is out of the question. Anyway, who are these people who can just order us to be disposed of like this? Where do they come from?"

"A man named Meredith Jordon is the 'who'. Based normally in Paris the 'where'. Why should I not order that you all be placed in protected custody?"

"Because I for one would raise a stink you would not believe," said Abby. As long as I am free to act I am not about to let a bunch of thugs dictate my movements, my life.... or my death for that matter. If they wish to continue what they are doing then, I will do all in my power to stop them in whatever way is necessary." She sat back, blushing at the passion of her outburst.

Donny said "Thanks, Abby, I could not have expressed it better myself. I can see it would be sensible for the parents to be protected. But for Abby and me, well. I think we have shown we can look after ourselves so just leave us out of any scheme you have in mind that involves keeping us under wraps.

"Now, this Meredith Jordon. What does he do for a living and where in Paris does he operate from? Secondly, why have the police allowed him to keep operating?"

"Jordon is your average worst nightmare." Jonathan said quietly. "He runs one of the most efficient smuggling operations in Europe, anything from drugs to information. If there is money in it, he is also. His right-hand man is the man Harry Sanders, an east-end thug with brains. His girlfriend was the woman Felicia Wagram. She was the woman who died in the argument with Rupert Dawson while you were in Crete."

"Of course. I knew the name was familiar." Abby interjected.

"If," said Jonathon, "Harry thinks you had something to do with her death, it would explain why they keep after you. The other explanation is, that 'Merry' Jordon' as he is known, simply does not like loose ends. That could be it. He is renowned for his quirky vicious temper and outrageous cruelty. Not a nice man to cross and you did cost him a lot of money. At least a million we estimate."

Chapter Ten

Neither of the pair told their parents that they were going hunting rather than back to University. Both decided that there were good reasons to keep that little piece of information to themselves. They both returned to their respective tutors and told them of their decision to take time out. They also requested that they kept the information to themselves if it was at all possible. Both suggested that their parents were so protective they would not approve of their projected South American trip to help orphaned Peruvian children.

They met at the boat once more for two reasons. The first being that it was their only source of weapons. Second that they needed to get into France armed, somehow without detection, and have a place to lay low where they would not need to stay in a hotel.

It was in Cobh itself that they landed lucky. Having established their credentials by sailing the ketch from Crete to Cobh, they were welcomed into the group of sailing enthusiasts that was regularly gathered at the local yacht club.

Mentioning that they were planning a trip to Paris and needing somewhere to stay there, one of the regulars approached them with a suggestion that they spoke to one of the members who was looking for someone to deliver his cruiser to Le Havre. The arrangement was to meet in the lounge of the local hotel.

Donny spotted their man as agreed, introduced himself and sat down.

John FitzGerald ran an electronics business in the City of Cork. His 56 foot cruiser was moored out in the bay, gleaming white upperworks and navy blue hull a picture of seagoing elegance. Powered by two big diesels she could hit 25 knots, and handle most of the weather likely to come her way. He wanted the boat delivered to Le Havre, intending to take it upriver to Paris in time for an autumn cruise through the rivers and canals to the south of France.

John FitzGerald was a big man, over six feet tall and fit-looking with it. Donny thought he was a former rugby player, and suggested as much.

FitzGerald looked at him with steady blue eyes. "I see you have your father's ability to sum people up." He grinned. "You didn't know I knew your father, did you?"

Donny looked puzzled. "Frankly, no. How do you know him?"

FitzGerald laughed. "I went to Southampton University. I got involved in a rather boisterous night out with the rugby team. To cut a long story short, your dad got me out of what could have been a nasty situation. I have never forgotten. So what was it you wanted to see me about?"

Donny said "We have just laid up our ketch in Cobh and heard that you wanted your boat delivered to Le Havre. Since we were heading for Paris ourselves, we were planning to hire a boat to sail upriver to Paris. We wondered if you would like us to take it over for you."

John FitzGerald sat back in his seat, and considered the young man seated opposite him. "It's a big boat to handle, you know. What size is your ketch, forty foot?" At Donny's nod he took a drink from his glass. Then he sat up having made up his mind.

"I intend sailing down to the Riviera through France next summer. I really need to get the boat to Paris. If you could see your way to taking it the whole way it would suit me and save you looking for another boat for the river trip. If you agree we will have a deal."

"We will need to stay on the boat for three weeks in Paris, as we have a course to study at the Sorbonne before we travel on."

"Well, if you take the *Ballymore* there, provided you are clear by August, you can use the boat for your stay in Paris."

Donny looked keenly at John FitzGerald "You provide the fuel and food. We'll deliver her for nothing. We'll leave her ready to walk into. Deal?"

FitzGerald slapped Donny's hand. "Deal."

He produced a wad of euro notes from his pocket, and peeled off a bunch and held it out to the man opposite. "The tanks are full. If you refuel in Le Havre it should take you all the way to Paris." He took a fuel credit card from his pocket and said, "Leave this in the drawer of the chart table, and the keys in the office at the mooring."

He called the waiter and a second round of drinks appeared. Abby arrived as Mrs. FitzGerald came in to join her husband. After introductions all round, John FitzGerald said to his wife, "Well timed both of you. We have just agreed that these two people will be taking the boat to Paris. Let's go and find dinner somewhere."

* * *

The waters of the Channel were blue in the sunshine. The big cruiser burbled along effortlessly at a steady 16 knots. Abby, at the wheel on the flying bridge, allowed the auto pilot to control the speed and direction while she lay out along the bench seat enjoying the sunshine.

"Wake up, lazybones. Come and get it." The voice of Donny from the main cabin below brought her to her feet. As she descended the stairs she called back, "About time, I'm starving. I thought the service would be better on this gin palace. It seems as bad as it was in the *Swallow.*"

The food was laid out on the table that was placed behind the lower control position, so they could keep their eye on the situation while they ate. The bottle of wine was open and ready to pour.

Abby gazed at the steaming steak pie that was the centerpiece of the offering. As she looked up at Donny, she raised an eyebrow questioningly.

"The Fitz family obviously have a weakness for the local butcher's steak pie." Donny answered the unspoken question.

"Thank goodness for that." Abby said "I thought there for a minute that I was playing footsie with a closet Chef."

"Anyone that can boil a kettle can heat up a readymade pie." Donny quipped, "But don't write me off completely. The Scottish Pancakes are all my own work." He indicated the plate of gently cooling pancakes on the side table, waiting to be eaten later.

As they ate, they chatted generally, both keeping an eye out for approaching boats and ships. The radar was set to the five mile range and it was clear of any real problems all round.

"I'm getting the impression that you are setting me up for something, the food, the wine." The direct gaze was once more turned on Donny. "So, what's the catch? What am I being let in for?"

They were sitting back still sipping their wine having made a large dent in the steak pie.

Donny reached across and tipped her chin up. "You are a suspicious lady, Abby Marshall. Why should there be a hidden agenda? I enjoy spoiling you. I thought you would have realized that by now."

She leaned forward and kissed him gently on the lips. "You're a smooth talker, Donald Weston, but I can see through the flannel. Let's have the story. I can take it."

Donny made his mind up. "Right, here it is. I have been trying to think of a way to put this that won't send you off like a rocket. I am worried about the excursion in Paris. I think you should think seriously about staying out of it. Leave it to me." He held his hands up to stop her immediate protest. "Please let me finish. I have tried to play things between us as low-key as I can. You made it clear the last time the subject came up that you were not committed to a future together. My problem is that I..." He hesitated looking for the words, then, "What I mean is that I know I love you. I couldn't bear it if something happened to you because of my insistence on going for this man, Merry Jordon." He stopped, head down leaving the words hanging in the air between them.

Abby moved over beside him and kissed him. "That is probably the nicest proposal that anyone has not made to me. The answers are 'yes' and 'no'. Yes, I will marry you. No, I will not let you go into the lion's den without me. From now on it's you and me together all the way, win or lose. Got it?"

Donny looked as if he had been stunned "Married. Proposal.....but I didn't say....."

Abby cut him off putting her finger over his lips "Are you trying to get out of marrying me, after taking advantage of me, on several occasions I may add? Is that what you are saying?"

She sat back and skewered him with her steady gaze.

"Of course not, I. I. Oh, I don't know what I said." He stuttered.

"So you do want to marry me then?" Abby was relentless.

"Of course I do. But...." Again Abby stopped him before he could say what he was about to say.

"You want to marry me, but. What does that mean? You are putting conditions on it now. You will only marry me if, if what?"

Donny gave up and threw his hands in the air. "I give up. I want to marry you, without conditions. Let's decide how we are going to tackle Mr. Jordon when we get to Paris."

Satisfied Abby sat back, happy that she had overcome that little problem. She had actually received a proposal of marriage from the man she was going to marry anyway. And, incidentally, made it clear she had no intention of letting Donny tackle the villains alone.

* * *

They managed to cross the busy trade routes that run the length of the Channel without incident and arrived in Le Havre safely.

Staying overnight in Le Havre they enjoyed an excellent meal in a quiet Auberge out of town. The hired car was seriously filled with provisions from a visit to the Auchan Hypermarket on the outskirts of the city taking care of the provisioning arrangements for the journey up the Seine, to Paris at least. By the time they fell into the huge bed in the master's suite on board both were exhausted. They were asleep as soon as their heads hit their respective pillows.

The trip up the river to Paris was idyllic for them both. They made no attempt to break records. Just cruised the river for four days reaching Paris in the early evening and mooring up for the last time on this voyage. Tomorrow was the beginning of a serious and dangerous exercise. From now on they would need to be watchful and armed wherever they went. Neither had any illusions about the difficulties they faced or the dangers they were in. Their only clues were the name of Merry Jordon and Harry, the man they had missed in Crete.

Chapter Eleven

Harry Sanders was upset. That was putting it mildly. Having discovered his partner, Felicia, had been killed in Crete soon after he had himself left, his first inclination had been to return immediately to find her killer and take his rage and frustration out on whoever it was.

This did not suit his boss who decided he needed him in Paris, while he set up a series of contacts with a new supplier of crack cocaine. As far as Harry was concerned any two of Jordon's other men could have done the job without his presence. Harry decided that the days of Merry Jordon's life were numbered. His apartment in the third arrondissement was comfortable and it was his own. If he left Jordon's employ he would not need to move. He looked at himself in the mirror. Who was kidding who? Jordon would not allow him to give notice and leave. It didn't work that way in this business. Feet first with a bullet in the head if he was lucky. Otherwise long and painful, it would just depend on how Jordon was feeling at the time. It was either kill or be killed in this game.

He crossed to the bar on the other side of the lounge. The front panel was decorated with intricate etched woodwork. He touched a particular place on the design and the panel slid back exposing a rack of weapons. The top row was made up of hand guns, below were two smg's one Uzi, and an MP40, a relic of WW2.

Below was another relic, a Scope mounted Lee Enfield .303 calibrated sniper rifle, and below that a modern Barratt sniper rifle.

He selected his weapon of choice for the city, a Walther PPK. He had never used one until he saw his first James Bond movie. In it Bond had been separated from his favorite gun by M's orders. Curious, Harry had acquired one, admittedly a later model. He was impressed enough to adopt it for everyday use.

A similar model of his gun was at present moving at a steady pace down the Rue Rivoli on its way to the Louvre. In the handbag alongside the gun was the usual collection of things to be found in most women's handbags. This particular one had a passport in the name of Abigail Marshall, said woman holding hands with Donald Weston. Neither had a clue where to start looking for the object of their visit. They had arrived in Paris two days ago and were now waiting for contact from Jonathon Glynn, who had been sworn to secrecy about their information request. The Louvre was a way to pass the time whilst waiting.

Neither had visited Paris before. For the moment everything was new and interesting. Both had been captivated by the feeling of freedom from the tensions of the past months. The impression of anonymity they felt by being in the centre of a completely strange place, surrounded by strangers, gave a false feeling of security that could be dangerous. Donny was aware of this but didn't have the heart to disillusion Abby too soon.

When they returned to the boat later that evening, they decided to go to the café just along the quay for a quiet drink, and to watch the strollers walking along the riverside. They had got to meet a few of the young people who used the café. When they entered several of them waved hello.

In the corner unnoticed by the others sat a small man quietly watching the group of young people. He was making no particular effort to do anything apart from pass the time and watch the way the bodies of the girls, particularly, moved under their skimpy short skirts and cropped tops. Robert Carton wasn't a pervert. He had convinced himself of that, just a normal male with normal instincts and desires. He had found that being short had its drawbacks. He wasn't fat or ugly, so why was it he had no luck with women? So far, if he didn't pay he didn't play. Since his working partner was always pulling birds and bringing them back for, as he put it, lust sessions, he spent a lot of time frustrated and abusing himself to the background music of Big Mike's lovemaking in the next room. He was in fact in the café because Mike was already in the apartment they shared. He really did not wish to share another evening listening to the music of creaking bedsprings.

As he sat there brooding quietly over his beer he heard snatches of conversation from the group around him. The odd word penetrated his mood. He became aware that the couple that had just arrived was speaking accented French. In fact they were English. They had just crossed from Ireland and brought their boat upriver to Paris.

He listened with more interest as he studied the English pair. The man was tall, athletic-looking with a lithe relaxed manner and obviously a good relationship with his partner. She was something else now he looked at her. Surrounded as he was by good-looking young people he had assumed she was just another girl. Now as he studied her, he realized that this one was in another class. His mouth went dry and he licked his lips, picturing taking her home on his arm and walking in on Mike and his floozies with that stunner beside him. He drifted off in a daydream, gaining a foot in height in his own mind.

His dream was roughly interrupted when the word Crete came into the conversation. What was it he knew about Crete? Where had he heard about Crete recently? At the back of his mind an elusive memory was gradually coming back to him. He dismissed it temporarily and concentrated on the conversation he was overhearing. The English couple, Donny and Abby, were discussing sailing in the Mediterranean, with an Australian tow-headed youth whose arm was draped round the shoulders of a small busty French girl with dark hair.

Donny was saying, "We sailed from Iraklion five weeks ago and had no problems handling the boat between us. She is a forty foot ketch but there was nothing we couldn't handle between us. You should have no problems provided you both know what you are doing. Have you sailed much?"

"I know my way round the east coast of Queensland. I've crewed and skippered several different boats out to the big reef, motor and sail."

"I would say you'll have no real problems then." Donny concluded.

Behind them Robert Carton had heard enough. He remembered where he had heard about Crete and two young people the boss wanted to talk to. Outside the café on the sidewalk he opened his cell phone and dialed Mike at the apartment.

Mike was not pleased to be disturbed amid his personal grooming operation with the two women currently enjoying free association in the big double bed.

"What?" Mike's voice growled down the phone. Robert felt the sweat start at the tone of his voice. He had guessed that Mike would not be pleased at the interruption. It was too late now. "Mike, it's Robert," he began...

"I know who you are, idiot. I've got eyes, what the fuck do you want?"

"That message from Harry Sanders. I think I've got the two people he wants spotted." Robert's voice almost cracked in his excitement. If he was right, what he knew would be worth plenty.

There was a pause on the other end of the phone. Then, "Tell me!"

"I was just having a beer in the café on the Rive Gauche, you know the place where all the students hang out, when I heard this couple talking."

"Get on with it. What happened?" Mike was impatient but his mind was working. Doing a favor for Harry Sanders could be worth plenty. Harry was a coming man and had a lot of pull with Merry Jordon.

"They were talking about how they brought a boat from Crete the length of the Med.' I remembered that Harry was looking for two youngsters sailing a boat in the Med last heard of in Crete. Remember the rumor was that he lost his woman in Crete along with one of his boys. It should be worth something, shouldn't it?"

"Where are these two now?"

Robert panicked. He swung round and looked through the window of the café, straight into the eyes of the young man he was discussing. His first reaction was relief that they had not disappeared since he had left the café. Then he realized that the person he was looking at had noticed him and was rising to his feet.

"I've got to go. They've seen me," he said hurriedly. He cut Mike off, turning to run along the waterside away from the café and a confrontation with the athletic-looking young man.

As he swung away from the lights of the café he realized there was somebody standing in the way. He automatically put out his hand to brush the person aside and felt the soft mound of a woman's breast under his hand. The next thing he knew was the sudden odd look of the cobble stone that was perhaps 15 millimeters from his right eye, kept that distance away by his cheekbone which was painfully pressed against the neighboring cobblestone. How had he got here? Still not quite with it he pushed himself upright, first to his knees. There, in front of his face, were a pair of tanned legs, as he raised his eyes they seemed to carry on upwards endlessly, finally reaching the denim mini skirt surmounted by the crisp white blouse stretched interestingly by the breast that he had so briefly grasped.

His progress upward was accelerated roughly by the fist grasping the neck of his shirt and yanking him to his feet. It was so unfair he had been enjoying the view from his place on the ground. The memory of that soft breast had just begun to percolate through the fog.

"Wha...what's happening? What are you doing?" His voice sounded odd even to him.

"Why don't you tell us?" The harsh Australian accent made him even more uneasy as he struggled to escape the vice-like grip on his shirt collar. He looked around and saw he was surrounded by what seemed to be the entire group of people from within the café. The woman in front of him was waiting to hear what he had to say.

"I was just off home to my girlfriend. As I turned I believe I must have bumped into this lady and tripped." His voice trailed off as he realized that the group around him was not amused by his explanation.

The smooth voice of the Englishman interrupted his thought at that moment "Who were you talking with on the cell phone?"

"I told you, my girl friend. I was just telling her I would be home soon." Robert's voice sounded more normal now but his face reflected his unease.

"Bollocks!"The contemptuous voice of the Australian was reinforced by the tightening of the collar of the shirt choking the unfortunate man, causing him to start gasping for breath and struggle against the constricting collar. "Now, tell us, you bastard. Who you were talking to? You snoop around the café. I've seen you several times before eying up the girls. Just give me some good reason why I should not just give you over to the police as a pervert, you little squit."

"Please," gasped Robert."I was not doing anything. I was just having a quiet beer before going home. Please my girlfriend will be waiting."

A voice from within the crowd said, "What girlfriend? You haven't had a girlfriend for all the years I've known you. You hire one when you can afford it. I should know you've tried to get your hand up my skirt often enough ever since we were at school together." The speaker was the dark-haired girl who had been sitting with the Australian when they were talking to Donny and Abby.

She turned to the group. "Meet Robert Colbert, pimp and runner for the local mob, friend of Big Mike, the Hood. At least, he spends most of his time hanging round trying to get leavings from Mike's table. He is a local weasel who will sell his mother to you for the price of a cocaine hit, that he doesn't use by the way. The coke will go to stunning some poor bitch into servicing him. No self respecting whore would look at him otherwise. This is a sad looking relic of what once was a sad looking child. He told the police that his mother was stealing and spent the reward on sweets." This tirade was followed by a breathless silence as the crowd took in this interesting piece of local knowledge. Then almost as one the group seemed to look at Robert with renewed interest. Rather in the way people looked at a bowl of maggots, with a sort of distant disgust. As the Australian afterwards put it 'like a fart in a church'.

Robert was gradually turning puce as he labored to breathe so his captor eased the pressure, allowing him to gasp and gulp in air. "Now, you horrible little man, tell us who you were really calling?"

He reached out and plucked the phone from Robert's pocket. He pressed the connect switch once and then a second time. The redialed phone produced an answer from a gravelly-voiced man. Presumably thinking Robert was calling, he promised to settle up in the morning and slammed the phone down.

The stunned silence was broken by Abby. "Oh dear. I think perhaps you have woman trouble. If that was your girl friend's home you have a cuckoo in the nest. The entire group burst out laughing while Robert cringed inwardly.

Donny took the phone and stuck it in his pocket as the figure of Robert Carlton was jostled and pushed, until he was able to get away from the good humored crowd.

Donny looked over to Abby and nodded to the river. She nodded back and shortly afterwards, having joined forces on the riverbank they strolled back to the boat mooring. Not at any time had they mentioned the fact that they were staying on a boat. Donny could not resist having a good look round when they boarded to see if there were any signs of a watcher or follower.

With the curtains drawn they sat and discussed the events of the evening. "I think we are getting closer." Abby said thoughtfully. That little creep phoned his boss to tell him we were here. I would bet on it. The only person interested in us would Harry Saunders and/or his boss."

Donny considered for a few minutes then got up and put the kettle on. From the galley he called, "I think you are probably right. The little creep was staring at me all the time he was talking on his cell phone. I became aware of him in the café when we were talking about sailing from Crete. He seemed to suddenly prick up his ears."

"We should consider moving away from here. It would not be too difficult to find out where we are staying. Mr. FitzGerald would be upset if he found the boat in a mess because we attracted the wrong sort of attention."

Abby's dry comment shook Donny. She was right. They would be easy to trace if someone really put their mind to look. They had not really tried too hard to cover their tracks.

Over coffee they discussed where they should move to without leaving a trail.

Donny picked up the phone and speed-dialed Jonathon. After a succession of clicks and buzzes his voice came through loud and clear. "Jonathon!"

"Donny here. Abby and I are in Paris. We think we have been spotted by Harry's man. Can you suggest a quiet spot where we can keep low for a while?"

"Home seems a good idea in the circumstances, but obviously that would be too simple. In Paris, my apartment is in Pigalle." He reeled off the address. "The keypad code is 1815. Got all that?" At Donny's 'yes', he continued. "I'll be back in Paris by tomorrow, stay low until I get there." The phone clicked and the hiss of static indicated that the connection had been broken. Donny put the phone down. "Get packed. We're off. Now!"

Chapter Eleven

It was at least one hour later that the visitor called. A shadow flitted across the deck towards the saloon door. Its progress was interrupted by the cold voice that spoke from the darkness beneath the overhang that sheltered the saloon doors from the effects of direct sunlight. "Stop, and tell me what you are doing here. The gun is loaded by the way." The words were reinforced by the click of the cocking hammer of the Walther automatic that showed briefly in the reflected light of the from the Marina pontoon.

The intruder stopped to weigh up the chances, then the woman spoke. "I was looking for two young people whom I was told were staying here on the boat." The breathy sexy voice was almost an invitation. It sent a shiver up the spine of the holder of the gun.

"Do you always call on people in the dark?" The voice did not display any emotion.

"I was hoping to surprise them." The woman suggested.

"Well, they beat you to it. They've gone without leaving a forwarding address. If you don't believe me knock on the door and see if anyone answers. I've been here for the past hour and there has been no sign of them. Check with the Marina manager next time. It will save you a trip."

The gun disappeared out of the faint light and a rustle of movement was followed by silence, and the woman realized that the watcher had left. *Who was he? What was he doing here?*

From the shadows on the quay Donny watched as the woman strolled round the deck of the big cruiser checking the windows then left the boat, stripping off the black overall that covered her short summer dress. Taking a carrier bag from the pocket she stuffed the overalls into the carrier and strode off down the pontoon.

Satisfied he had got the message across Donny quietly left the Marina and returned to Abby at Jonathon's apartment.

At the Marina Office the woman leant through the door. "The *Ballymore,* the big cruiser parked on the 'A' pontoon, I thought there was a young couple staying on the boat?"

The man sat in the office drinking beer, grinned. "Nice ass. Yeah, they left today, didn't leave a forwarding address. Sorry to see her go."

The woman grimaced at the man's lascivious tone. She was tempted to tip the chair up dumping the man, beer and all on the floor. But decided otherwise, left with nod at the attendant, and disappeared into the dark.

* * *

Jonathon Glynn sat back in his chair and sighed. There was a lot going on all at once and he was beginning to feel hassled. Having loaned his apartment to Donny and Abby, he had called in a favor and borrowed the flat of a colleague who was currently on leave. He would contact them tomorrow but meanwhile he reached for his telephone and dialed a number.

* * *

Donny and Abby were lying cuddled up close to each other in Jonathon's big bed.

"That was a close call, I think," Abby said.

The only answer she got was a grunt as Donny snuggled closer under the warm duvet.

"Do you think the gang are on to us?" Abby persisted, wriggling in Donny's grip to try and get an answer.

This time she got a gurgle and an answering wriggle with definite intentions behind it.

Giving up for the moment at least Abby turned over with her hands reaching out. "All right. Let's see what you've got then."

Both then collapsed in helpless laughter and the inquest into the evening's events was deferred at least until the next morning.

* * *

Harry Sanders was reaching the point of no return with Mr. Merry Jordon. The latest enterprise required the use of complete strangers to carry out what Harry considered to be a very basic operation. Of course the whole thing had been botched and Harry was getting the blame.

The raised, far from merry, voice of his boss was at the highest decibel level which meant that the boss had actually lost money on the enterprise. Part of the reason for the screams of the boss was the complete lack of any emotion on Harry's behalf.

Finally he reached his limit. Drawing his automatic he stuck it in the shouting face before him with the comment, "Suck this!"

Merry became silent immediately, then carefully. "Now. Harry. Don't get your knickers in a knot, you know I'm only joking. Just letting off steam. That's all." He backed away from Harry's menacing gun, both hands up.

Harry looked at him weighing up his choices. "Shall I or shall I not?"

He lowered his gun, thumb on the hammer to ease the spring. Then he uncocked it.

They say that in life there are a series of pivotal moments. Maybe the offhand purchase of a winning lottery ticket, the last minute change of a flight that never arrived, the fatal step off the pavement into the path of a truck whilst distracted by a pretty woman.

Life they say is a lottery. Merry thinking the storm was over, did what came naturally to him. He shouted at Harry to stick his gun up his arse, and get back to business.

Two things happened. Harry stopped uncocking his weapon. He shot Merry between his open mouth and his nose. His legend was enhanced by the accuracy and the neatness of the shot. Though Harry never admitted it the location of the wound was fortuitous. Harry had just lifted the gun and fired in the general direction of Merry.

Well, there he was, smoking gun in hand, when the others rushed in. "He went too far and blew it. Stupid prick!"

The other men just stared and, conspicuously, didn't go for their own guns. Harry carried far too much respect for that. Besides his gun was in his hand already.

Harry put the gun away. He turned to the five men standing looking at him. "Right. I've taken over operations as from now. Any objections?"

The men shuffled their feet and looked at each other until one stepped forward."We've got no objections, Boss. We were all getting worried about Merry going too far. We're just as pleased that the problem has been solved."

"Right. Get the body out of the way. Frisk him first. Then dump him in the river." He turned and looked at the woman who had been waiting for Merry. "Have you got anything else to do at the moment?"

She shook her head while Harry looked her up and down, approving of her. "What's your name?"

"Marianne;" she said. He nodded to the bedroom next door and followed her, closing the door behind him.

Marianne moved in the following day

* * *

There was tension in her eyes as she ran down the street her hair flying out like a red flag behind her. She stumbled and recovered. After a quick look behind her she ran on, her breath coming in gasps as the pace began to tell.

She rounded the corner and ran straight into the arms of the tall man walking toward her. He staggered with the impact, but managed to keep his feet.

Jonathon studied the girl in his arms with interest. Her striking red hair surrounded a rather pale face. The grey green eyes were looking startled at the moment but not afraid.

He realized that he was still clutching her close in his arms, suddenly aware of the contours of her slender figure and her faint perfume. He straightened and loosened his grip.

"Sorry. Is there something wrong? Is someone chasing you?"

The girl stood upright and looked at him directly as she straightened her clothing. "There was. But I think I lost them." She was thinking quickly. "I think they wanted to mug me. You know steal my handbag or something. I did not wait to see. I pushed one into the other and ran."

Jonathon stepped to the corner and carefully looked round. There was nothing happening there. He turned back and, as he did, heard the girl gasp. Two men were walking determinedly towards them. They must have cut the corner off, trying to catch her. Jonathon took the girl's arm and spun her round the corner out of sight of the two men who had started to run.

"Quick, this way. He took her hand and ran down the street to the first alley on the right. Turning down the alley he stopped suddenly at the first door and tapped a four figure combination into the lock. With a click the door opened. He thrust the girl inside closing the door behind him. They heard voices as the men stopped baffled at the disappearance of their quarry. Jonathon took the girl's hand once more and led her down the dark passageway to the stairs. He led her up to the first floor of the building and, on the landing, produced a key to open the door on the left.

The girl walked warily though the door into the apartment.

Jonathon flung his coat on to the clothes rack inside the door and called over his shoulder, "Coffee, or would you like something stronger?" He moved into the small kitchen without waiting to see if the girl had followed.

"Coffee will be good, thank you." As the tall figure disappeared into the kitchen she thought about this man who had not turned a hair at the events of the past few minutes. He was nice looking rather than handsome, dark hair, blue eyes. From her encounter she had noticed that he was pretty fit, taller than her 5ft 6ins, perhaps six feet?

After a short period of clatter Jonathon emerged from the kitchen with a tray on which stood a coffee pot with steam rising from the spout, two cups and a plate with biscuits. "Sugar's on the sideboard if you need it." His calm breezy manner was reassuring to the girl who took off her coat and hung it on the rack next to Jonathon's.

Seated with the coffee in front of her, Jonathon had a proper look at his catch. He found that she in her turn was looking at him.

"I am Jonathon Glynn. This is my apartment. I promise you I did not set out this evening with the intention of luring a beautiful young lady to join me here. Though I have no intention of throwing you out against your will." His smile as he made his declaration made it clear that he was not a threat.

She studied him with steady eyes making no attempt to disguise the fact. Then she spoke in a low cultured voice, with an accent, but in perfect English. "My name is Carol Varenne. I live here in Paris in Rue Haussmann. I am in business as an accountant.

Jonathon did not push her. She appreciated the fact that this rather nice looking Englishman was not a threat. He was sensitive, making allowance for the fact that she had had a shock and willing to let her explain in her own time. She thought of her fiancé, Robert. In this situation he would be phoning the Police and demanding action in a flurry of anger and complaint. The calm relaxed man in front of her was not only reassuring. He was also rather attractive. At this thought she felt a twinge of guilt over Robert. But immediately shrugged it off, remembering that he was currently in the south working on a project for his employers.

"I have been working on the accounts of a rich business man who lives here in the city. He has interests all over the world. I contacted him recently over some odd discrepancies in his portfolio. To my surprise he became very angry when I pointed them out.

"Up until now he has always been the perfect gentleman in all his dealings with me. In fact my fiancé is employed by him. But on this occasion he turned on me and shouted that it was none of my business to intrude in his private affairs and to stick to business in future. I had no idea what he meant or in fact what he was talking about. So I told him to stuff his accounts, to find someone else to deal with them and stormed out.

"I sent his accounts back to his office the following morning and decided that I would continue with my other accounts. Meanwhile seek other business.

"That was two days ago. Since then I noticed I was being followed. Because my fiancé was away I cleared my desk computer and transferred everything onto my laptop, and back-up disks. I left my apartment quietly and went to stay in the apartment of a friend. She is a flight attendant who spends most of her time away from Paris. I keep her key, you see." She looked at Jonathon who nodded understandingly.

Carol continued pouring out her story to this man whom she just met but who oddly made her feel safe and who listened. Something Robert had not learned to do during the several months of their engagement.

"Having lost all trust in my client, despite having returned his paperwork, I actually deposited all the copied accounts on disk into my bank. I felt insecure and uneasy about the people following me. So I downloaded his records onto my iPod and deleted them from the laptop, which is in my friend's apartment. The iPod is in my bag. I came out to get something to eat as there was nothing in the fridge. The men spotted me when I left the café where I had dinner. You know the rest."

Jonathon stood and walked over to the side-board and collected a bottle of brandy and two glasses. Placing them on the table between them he looked up and raised an eyebrow.

Carol nodded. He poured two drinks and passed one of the glasses to her.

The both sipped the brandy then Jonathon spoke. "Who were you working for?"

"Meredith Jordon of Jordon International Trading," she said quietly. "He has offices in Rue St Germaine."

Jonathon nodded silently. Then, "I'm afraid you have upset a very dangerous man. Merry Jordon is well known in certain circles, but not for legitimate business. Whatever his public interests are, his private business is criminal. Merry, as he is known, has his finger in everything from industrial espionage to murder, from fraud to extortion, robbery to prostitution. He is credited with several killings personally, though he has never been convicted."

Carol had gone white at his comment. "But he......"

"Covered his tracks well?" Jonathon completed her comment.

The couple sat quietly, each occupied with their own thoughts. Then Carol said, "You seem to know a lot about all this?" She looked at him quizzically.

"I am a security consultant. It's my business to know." Jonathon answered.

This seemed to satisfy Carol who sat back on the settee and sipped at her brandy once more.

After a period of silence Jonathon spoke. "I think you would be better to stay here overnight and we can sort out more suitable arrangements tomorrow. My nephew and his girlfriend stays here occasionally. She is about you're size. She leaves some clothes here, just in case." He added quickly as he noticed her raised eyebrow.

Carol looked at him steadily for a few moments. She smiled and said, "For someone who has just picked up a woman off the street, you are remarkably trusting, From my point of view I accept your offer with relief. I feel safe here and I am suddenly very tired." She yawned "I feel I could sleep for a week."

Jonathon rose to his feet took her hand and hauled her up from the settee. She swayed and rested briefly against his chest with her head on his shoulder. Then in response to his urging she allowed him to lead her into the second bedroom in the apartment. The bed was already made up and ready as always for unexpected visitors. Jonathon pointed out the towels and the shared bathroom, and left her standing by the bed, closing the door quietly behind him.

Before he went to bed he looked in on Carol as she lay sound asleep in the darkened bedroom. He smiled to himself as he closed the door. There was something about the redheaded woman he could not put his figure on. Whatever it was it excited him. He had not been excited by a woman for a long time.

* * *

Having returned from the previous night in Jonathon's apartment Donny and Abby had been handing over the boat to the agents. The van containing their effects, including the weapons they had with them stood on the quay waiting for them to finalize the inventory with the agent for John Fitz-Gerald. Abby waited in the passenger seat of the van idly watching the people wandering along the quay eyeing the boats.

As Donny and the agent stepped from the boat to the shore she noticed the increased interest of one of the wanderers. It was not something she would have noticed in the past as she was only too happy to admit. But since the world turned upside down and she had begun her association with Donny she was inclined to take a rather more cynical view of the world in general. The sharp look followed by his careful re-examination of Donny and the agent as they walked down the quay caught her attention. She slipped out of the door on the side away from the watcher and distanced herself from the van before running up to Donny, kissing him on the cheek. It gave her the opportunity to whisper, "Tall man behind me, black shirt by the wall."

She stepped back and smiled at the agent. "All finished? You have been most efficient."

The agent, a young man in his early twenties blushed and shrugged. The beautiful young lady made him envious and embarrassed, but also pleased to have earned the compliment.

"Do you have your car with you?" She asked sweetly.

"I am afraid not, Mademoiselle. I came by the Metro today."

"Donny, it's such a beautiful day. Do you think we could ask M'sieu Garland to drive the van to his office. The garage is only round the corner from there. We could stay and enjoy the sunshine by the river. It is so lovely today."

Donny turned to the agent who was currently melting under the full effect of the Abby smile.

"M'siu?" Donny asked.

"Of course. I would be delighted to." The agent said accepting the keys discretely passed over by Abby who managed to touch his hand as she did so.

A second blush followed the first. He hastily walked over to the van and waving to the young couple drove off the quay in a cloud of smoke from the over revving engine.

Abby took Donny's hand and they strolled off down the quay in the opposite direction from the watcher.

"So, what was that all about?" Donny asked.

"What do you mean?" Abby said innocently.

"Don't give me the innocent look. I know when you are up to something. That poor man thinks he is ready to take my place in your affections, right?"

"Why on earth should you think that? Or should he for that matter?"

She took out the mirror from her small handbag and managed to check that the watcher was following them. He was now on his mobile phone.

"The watcher is on his mobile and following us. I did not want them wrecking the boat looking for us, or attacking that poor man to find out where we were going. Hence the man had to leave safely and the van was the solution." She looked up at Donny. "OK?"

He looked down at her and smiled, "Cute, brains and looks. What would I do without you?" He bent and kissed her with enthusiasm. It was Paris. Nobody took notice, except the watcher of course.

* * *

They collected the van from the rear of the Agency office and returned it to the hire company. The contents had been transferred to their Recreational Vehicle en route. They took great care to sweep the van for bugs using the little gadget provided by Jonathon. Nothing showed up but to cover all angles Abby had made her own way to the garage where Jonathon kept the RV.

It had been Jonathon's idea. He had acquired the RV some time ago, it was only because of the sudden need to find accommodation for Donny and Abby, that he recalled that it was there, available, and a real solution to their problem.

She brought it out to meet Donny for the transfer of their gear. She returned to the camp site and Donny joined her later having used public transport for the journey.

The camper was not new. It had been converted from a Ford transit high-top long-wheelbase van. The fittings were professionally fitted and the windows had been inserted by a body shop. Up until recently it had been part of the surveillance fleet operated by the UK security services. There were still certain of the features retained from that service history. The gun locker for one, the security system that included exterior surveillance cameras and the electric shock system that had been used in the past to discourage people from touching the van in anger.

The windows could be darkened at the touch of a button. The number plates worked on the principle of those on the James Bond Aston Martin. A selection of four complete numbers changeable at will, that automatically matched front and rear but with an extra feature that permitted the user to alter each number and letter individually if needed.

The vehicle had been put up for tender by the Security services and sold to the only bidder. Jonathon Glynn had bid £2000 for the vehicle, it was intended for use by a lady of his acquaintance. Due to a mistake in the tender office, his bid had been accepted as £200 only.

Jonathon had garaged the vehicle, only to discover that the lady had decamped with her former husband.

The discovery that only £200 had been paid, led to the realization of the mistake made by the disposal body. They had overlooked the particular attributes of this vehicle. The gross mileage had not reflected the level of maintenance. Nor did its apparent age reflect the superb condition that had been maintained. Compounding the error by misrecording the bid persuaded the Civil Service that it would be sensible to ignore the whole business rather than admit this inefficiency to the world at large.

Jonathon realized that this was the answer to Donny and Abby's problem. The RV meant that they were not tied to any particular place. They would be able to stop wherever they wanted provided there was room to park of course.

Chapter Thirteen

Harry Saunders was sitting quietly contemplating the computer screen in front of him. The place had been re-decorated since the passing of Merry Jordon. The brash colors favored by his erstwhile boss had been replaced by the more muted restful shades of magnolia, grey and green. The lights were softened with wall fittings to replace the ornate chandelier that had blazed down from the centre of the ceiling. The sale of the chandelier had funded the entire refurbishment of the apartment, with change. Harry chuckled to himself. There was no doubt that Merry had no taste. But he knew a bargain when he saw one.

On the screen before him was the agenda for an operation that he had in mind for some time. The basic plans were now decided. All he needed now was the recruitment of the personnel for the job. That could be the problem.

"Marianne, talk to me." He spoke in a normal easy tone, and returned to the screen.

After a few minutes he looked up and round the room. Marianne was curled up on the sofa texting on her mobile.

"Marianne, talk to me." He repeated.

Concentrating on her text Marianne ignored him.

Harry got up and walked over to her. He reached down and took the phone from her hand and threw it across the room with enough force to cause it to shatter apart against the far wall.

"What's that all about? I was just texting my mother." Marianne said angrily.

"Well, text her some other time. I was talking to you." He slapped her gently on the cheek his voice still quiet. But it scared the hell out of her. She was immediately contrite. "Sorry. Harry, I was miles away. What did you want?"

Harry returned to his chair in front of the screen. "I want you to get Peterman Dave to come here for a meeting. I have a job for him."

For the second time that day Marianne nearly lost it. She started to say "Don't be daf...t" and saw the look on Harry's face. "You mean it, don't you? Even after he shafted Merry over that espionage deal?"

"I mean it. He always fancied you. If anyone can bring him in, it's you."

"How am I supposed to do that? I haven't spoken to him for three months."

"Now, come on, girl. You know how. Flash your knickers. He'll be panting after you, ready to rip your clothes off before you reach the bedroom." Harry smiled. "I have confidence in you, remember. I have personal experience in these matters."

Marianne shrugged resignedly."I thought I was finished with all that. You told me I would not have to go back on the game."

As she started to get up Harry spoke once more.

"This is not the game, love. This is probably the biggest deal of all. It should sort out our future once and for all, alright." He stood and crossed to her taking her in his arms. "For us, love. It's for us. The last time, I promise."

She looked him in the eyes. "Promise. Can we get married then?" Her voice was wistful.

Harry smiled reassuringly. "Depend on it, my love. Depend on it."

Marianne skipped off to the bedroom to prepare, happy with Harry's promise.

Harry smiled to himself thinking 'stupid bitch'. She was the last person he would marry. He had plans for a much more suitable marriage when the time came. It was certainly not yet.

Peterman Dave was probably the best safe cracker in Europe, at least he thought so. He was always in demand for sensitive jobs, especially by the security services of the various Nations of the European Community. Despite the apparent concord between the countries there was no real trust between the nations. That was where Peterman came in. He could open and close safes without leaving any signs of his work. Copying documents and listing confidential material was simple mathematics to him. You pay the money, Peterman produced the results.

The problem for Harry was that Merry and Peterman had fallen out over a matter of money, and incidentally, Marianne. It was not because Merry was more attractive than Peterman. Neither man was what one might call attractive. Apart from the wealth that both owned, the only thing that Merry had that Peterman didn't was the charisma of power and sheer menace he generated.

His success with Marianne was down to the fascination created by his ruthless manipulation of others. Harry had replaced Merry. Harry had been a much more attractive proposition his body was in better shape. He still had the charisma though not quite so uncontrolled as his predecessor.

Though she was not particularly choosy she had hoped that Harry would keep her himself. Using her to attract Peterman was not what she had anticipated. But she shrugged, and went into the walk-in wardrobe to select the sort of restrained clothes that Peterman favored.

* * *

The demure looking girl that walked out of the bedroom gave Harry a shock. For a moment he considered getting someone else to lure Peterman back. Then he rationalized things. After all Marianne was his. She could be trusted for a job like this, so the moment passed.

He looked speculatively at the neatly dressed girl in the black pencil skirt and white blouse. The casual jacket round her shoulders accentuated the effect of her tied-back hair and stockinged legs, a secretary perhaps, a pretty secretary, out for lunch during her break. He nodded to himself there was no doubt she was a knockout in that outfit. A second of regret. He let her out of the apartment with a final admonition to look after herself. A most un-Harry like comment.

* * *

Jonathon and Carol sat and talked in the morning when she, at least, had had a good night's sleep. For Jonathon sleep had not come easy, disturbed as he was by the effect that Carol had had upon him.

Now, in the morning facing her, he realized that things had changed for him. He gave a moment's thought to her fiancé elsewhere in France. Then decided that if he worked for Merry Jordon, he must be aware that the man was a crook, since Carol had found out and left his service. He asked the question. "You mentioned that your fiancé works for Jordon. Does he know that you have found out that Jordon is a crook? Have you spoken to him about it?"

Carol looked up at him. She stopped eating her cereal and for a moment said nothing at all. Then she began to speak. "I rang him last night before I met you. I told him what I had discovered and what I had done. He was furious. He said I could cost him his job. What did it matter if the man sailed a little close to the wind. That was just business. He told me to ring up Jordon and apologize immediately."

For a moment she stopped speaking. Then "I told him that I thought he should tell Jordon to stick his business and look for work elsewhere. He was livid. How dare I talk to him like that? If that was my attitude then our relationship was over. He slammed the phone down and that was that."

"How do you feel about that?" Jonathon said coolly.

"I feel relieved. I think subconsciously I knew that we were finished anyway." She smiled a little sheepishly. "I feel a little guilty about it. But I cannot help the feeling of relief at the same time."

They both ate in silence and as they both finished, he rose to take the dirty dishes to the sink. Carol also rose and joined him at the sink. "I'll wash these up. Perhaps you would consider helping me collect my other things from the apartment. I cannot use it any more now I am no longer engaged to Rene. I will have to find another place to live anyway. I should move my stuff out hopefully whilst he is still away."

The front door of the apartment opened at that moment. Donny and Abby bundled through into the little lobby.

Seeing Jonathon, Donny said, "Hi. We've come to plan."

He stopped abruptly seeing Carol behind Jonathon. "Sorry I didn't realize you had a guest...." Abby bumped into him as his voice trailed off and Jonathon quickly stepped in "How could you, you weren't here when she came. Carol, this is Donny and Abby. They are friends of mine."

The two youngsters took off their coats and Abby put the kettle on.

Carol looked at Jonathon. "You'll be busy with them. I'll get off and find another apartment."

Jonathon held up his hand. "Stop. Get the coffee going. We'll have a council of war." At her puzzled look, he added, "All will come clear in a few minutes."

All four of them sat around the coffee table discussing the weather the shops and the traffic. Then Jonathon lifted his voice and called the other three to order. "We all have problems," he said. "Luckily, the problems are all about Merry Jordon, whom I can now confirm is dead. However the problem has not gone away. In many ways it has got worse because we now have to deal with Harry Saunders."

He explained that Harry Saunders was the former enforcer for the Jordon organization for years. He had been the man who organized all of the action on behalf of Merry Jordon. Unfortunately he had been the organizer of the attack on Donny's parents. The female who had died in the street at Iraklion had been his girlfriend. They were on the list as targets for the mob. Though there were no pictures being circulated, the descriptions were pretty accurate.

In Carol's case she was wanted because she knew where many of the skeletons were hidden, and was targeted accordingly.

"For both girls we need to change their hair, color and style. I think in the case of Donny, dress and hair color." He looked around at the group. "I want to impress on you all that the people we are involved with here are very dangerous. They have demonstrated that they are quite ruthless and money is no object. They will kill you all without mercy. Do you understand me?" He looked at Carol specifically. "In your case, Carol, you have no real experience of survival in these circumstances. I want you to promise me you will not go out on your own even after we have changed your appearance." He was looking very serious.

Carol looked at him and nodded, "Alright. I'll play the game. Let's get started!"

* * *

Harry Saunders looked at his men keenly. "So where did the bitch go? Nobody can just disappear from the street without going somewhere. Through the door of an apartment or maybe into a shop, I will accept. Thin air, I won't. Now go out to where she was last seen and make enquiries. Make out you're the Police. Use your bloody heads." He turned away from them and waited until all were gone before he spoke. "Alright, come out. Tell me how bad is it?"

Rene Picard came out from behind the screen hiding him from the gaze of the dismissed group of men and faced Harry. "It depends on whether she took copies of the records before she handed them back to Jordon. There is no record in the office or in our apartment. I have searched both. But she has her own laptop and there may be something on that. Until I get hold of it I cannot say."

"Your fiancée has possibly got enough evidence to put us all in jail. You don't know where she is. You have told her that it's all off between you. Is that a fair resume of matters to date?"

Rene looked miserable but nodded anyway.

"Has she taken her things from the apartment yet?" Harry asked.

"I don't think so. At least up until last night she hadn't."

"Right. What is your address; I'll have the boys keep an eye on things there in case she comes back for her gear."

Reluctantly Rene gave his address to Harry. He waited while one of his teams was told to go to the address and keep it under observation.

Twenty minutes later Harry's phone rang. The conversation was short and succinct. Afterwards Harry swung round to Rene who was sitting uncomfortably waiting to be dismissed.

For a moment nothing was said. Then Harry said, "She has been and gone. If you had mentioned this earlier we could have caught her."

Rene found he was relieved. Despite the fact that he had broken off the relationship with Carol and that to some extent the partnership had been a convenience, he had still felt some responsibility for her. Now she had cleared the apartment he could have a clear conscience if anything happened to her.

He was shocked into listening to Harry once more, when Harry shouted at him. "Do you hear me, idiot? If you had told us earlier we could have had her here and found out all we needed to know. As it is she has been and gone. We have no idea where she is now." He strode around the room angrily. While Rene kept his head down and tried to make himself as small as possible.

"Right. You get out of here and get your arse in gear. I want her found. Since you know her better than anyone else you should have the best chance. If you don't manage it, I suggest you make arrangements for your heirs and assignees because you will probably not make it into next week, if you take my meaning?"

Rene was out of the door of the apartment as fast as his legs would carry him. He did not stop until he was back at the apartment he had shared with Carol.

Once inside though. He closed and locked the door. He still did not feel safe and he wandered around the flat frantically trying to think of where Carol could or would have gone. It did not occur to him that she might have gone to the office they shared until he had finally sat down with a drink in his hand, still desperately trying to stop his knees quivering.

Gingerly he picked up the phone and speed dialed the office. "Hullo. Who is this?" The voice at the other end was unfamiliar. The French not quite right. "This is Bertrand. Put me on to either Rene or Carol if you please." There was a short delay then Carol's voice came on the phone "Carol here. Who is this, please?"

Rene was astonished for a moment. "Carol, it is Rene. Get out of there quickly. They are after you. They will k......" the voice stopped suddenly. Another voice came over the phone.

"Stay there, if you value your life." The voice was cold and hard, but the speaker was talking to silence. Carol had gone.

The office had been vacated in a hurry, Abby, who had answered the telephone along with Carol had cleared her desk and also Rene's, passing the contents down to Jonathon in the car below the window. Donny was at the corner keeping a lookout for visitors. When the call warning Carol came from Rene, the two girls both left through the window down the single fire escape stair at the rear of the building. Donny came on the run from the corner. He jumped into the car as Jonathon drove off. The men sent to the rear of the building missed them by seconds. The *Galaxy* rounded the next corner just before the men arrived to run up the fire escape.

"That was a little too close for comfort." Donny remarked. "They must have been on their way to the office already to have got there so early." He turned to the two girls. "How did you know?"

Carol explained about the warning from Rene. "They must have caught him at the apartment as he was making the call. I think it was not good news for Rene. He was cut off."

There were tears in her eyes as she recalled Rene's final words. Abby put her arm round her and gave her a hug. Jonathon who was driving, said, "It's time we got out act together. We'll get this stuff back to the apartment. Donny and I will look through the new stuff while you two get on with the cutting and dying. We can go to work on Donny when you're finished." There was no argument with that. They went directly to the apartment, cocooned within the interior of the Ford screened by the tinted windows.

* * *

Rene sat dejectedly back in Harry's apartment once more. His throat was sore where the hoodlum had nearly strangled him to try and stop him warning Carol over the phone.

Harry came in and listened to the report from the unhappy team leader. He waited until he had heard the whole story, then turned to look at Rene. "I didn't know you had it in you" he said quietly. "Well. Well. Who would have believed it? I had you pegged as a complete loser. Sell out your own mother to save your own skin and here you prove me wrong. He turned to the team that had taken Rene. "Take him out and drop him off at his home." He turned and left the room and Rene's captor jerked his head at Rene to come with him. Meekly Rene followed him out of the door.

By the time the small pa rty had reached Rene's apartment building, Rene was beginning to believe that he had got away with it. Sadly he was wrong. They dropped him off from the sixth floor, and the pavement was unforgiving.

Chapter Fourteen

Carol walked into the lounge of the apartment her dark-brown hair cut close to her head in a boyish style. The fine grey lamb's wool roll neck sweater draped her upper body over the tailored jeans that were tucked into her ankle boots.

Donny looked up hearing her enter, and gasped. Hearing him, Jonathon looked up in turn. He said, "Wow!"

Carol smiled a little hesitantly. "Will I do?"

Jonathon said, "You may not be recognized, but you certainly will be noticed." Donny was nodding in agreement as Abby came in.

Once again both males took a second look. Abby was dressed in a light cotton dress provided by Carol. Her restyled and tinted hair framed her face, the light and dark slightly tousled look suiting her normally serious face, giving her a jaunty slightly saucy look. The dress came down to her knee showing off her shapely legs to advantage. Her low heeled shoes finishing off the picture of a pretty Parisian girl. Beside Carol the two could be sisters.

Once more Jonathon commented with a smile. "Don't get me wrong, ladies. You were both worth a second look before. But now....." He turned to Donny "What do you think?"

"Wicked!"

Both girls blushed, then looked at each other and burst out laughing. Jonathon and Donny joined in, all four enjoying the relief from the build-up of tension over the past few hours.

Eventually Abby turned to Donny. "So what shall we do about you?"

Immediately all eyes were on Donny as they each studied him, making him feel as if he was a dummy in the window.

"The hair, trimmed crew-cut perhaps, darken a little. Clothes, definitely out of the jeans into chinos. Open necked shirt, no more T shirts. Crewneck sweater and sunglasses, perhaps regular glasses." Carol finished and turned to Abby. "What do you think?"

Abby looked at Donny with half-closed eyes then said, "With glasses. Yes. I agree."

"Hey. What about me? Don't I get a look in here?"

Both girls turned on him. "No!" They said together. "We can see what we are looking at. You can't."

Donny looked at Jonathon, who shrugged and held his hands up.

Leaving the girls to work on Donny, Jonathon went out shopping having taken a list of measurements with him. "Don't go out while I'm away. My neighbours might wonder what I was up to if they saw you. I would rather you all stayed in, out of sight for the moment."

* * *

Harry kept his temper but the rest of the men were all on edge, frightened that they would be on the wrong end of his bad mood and suffer for it. All were staying as far away from the base as possible. Marianne was the only one who could speak to him. That was only because she had ensnared Peterman Dave.

"So. What's the job then, Harry?" Peterman Dave was a small neat man who had learned his trade working for Chubb as an apprentice. They had given him the chance to work on all their rivals' locks at one time or another. The skills he had developed had stood him in good stead over the years. His small frame was as strong as a whip. He kept in trim with regular visits to the gym. Many a man had made the mistake of taking him for granted because of his size. They had learned their mistake the hard way.

Harry looked at him for a long moment. "This may well be beyond you. If it is tell me. I won't waste any more of your time or mine. Alright?"

"Tell me, Harry."

"Glauber kriegskanonegeschaft. Gmbh, in Essen have produced a weapon required by a client of mine. For reasons that won't interest you, they cannot obtain it directly from the factory. What I need is the drawings for the weapon without them knowing that we have copied them. I can offer you 500 grand Euros for the job."

"Make it Sterling, and you're on." Dave's voice was calm and even.

"You mean that. No arguing. No questions?"

"Don't waste my time, Harry. You know me well enough by now. I know the factory. Been there, done that. If it's on, the drawings will be with you within a week and no-one will know anything."

"Sterling. Done." Harry grinned. Good to do business with you, Dave.

* * *

Jonathon had left the other three in the apartment while he reconnoitered the area around Harry's headquarters. It was evident that there was some activity in the area. He was surprised to catch a glimpse of Peterman Dave leaving Harry's premises. It was a known fact that there was no love lost between the Jordon mob and the safe cracker. Still, Jordon had disappeared. Perhaps things were happening once more.

Tucking that thought away in the back of his mind, he concentrated on getting close enough to the building without raising the interest of the two heavies at the door.

He found that the camera covering the side of the building had been slightly displaced. With a little nudge would move even further out of line, leaving a dead spot along the side wall beneath the first floor window of Harry's apartment. He left the area at that point not wishing to make himself too obvious. The area was a mix of residential and business with plenty of activity during the day. It quietened down during the night. He would return during the evening, perhaps to install a listening device outside the window on the blind side of the building.

* * *

The bug had been carefully placed against the window of the room. The receiver recorder was attached to the wall behind a small bush. The recorder could be accessed by a signal from Jonathon's mobile phone. To the two listeners the conversation within the room came through loud and remarkably clear.

Back in the apartment the two girls, Donny and Jonathon sat round the table listening. Jonathon looked grave when he heard the subject of the conversation they were listening to.

"Whatever else we had in mind, this is too important to ignore. The weapon they are discussing is serious kit. I have to report to my masters about this. I may have problems getting them to believe this can be done."

Carol asked, "Why might they not believe you? It seems quite evident to me that they are confident they will succeed in getting the drawings of the thing."

"The security at the works is very strict. The company obviously thinks they can protect their software physically as well as electronically. I have suspected that their security has been breached in the past, simply because in one case at least another company produced a copy of one of their weapons in the past. There was no time for the thing to have been retroactively developed from a sample. No one believed me then. Why should they believe me now? I will try, but I think it will be down to me to stop or recover the drawings, before they can be passed on."

Abby said "Down to us! We have a problem with these people anyway. I would like to point out that there are personal scores to settle here. All of us have our lives under threat. Any action you elect to take against Harry and his mob will have to take us into account!"

Jonathon looked round the table. "I apologise. I was forgetting for a moment why we are all here. I will try to convince my boss. If I can't do it, then it will be up to us." He grinned, "The Four Musketeers, *all for one and one for all.*" They all laughed at this but there was a serious element about the whole matter. He turned to Carol. "You are the computer expert. Find out all you can about the company making the weapons and anything you can about the apartment block where Harry lives and works."

"Abby and Donny you will be out on the streets. Always go tooled up. Your disguise is good but you never know. Work together covering each other at all times. We cannot afford to lose either of you. I need to know all the haunts of Harry's men and any other premises they may regularly use. No risks please?"

"No risks, it is." Abby answered for them both.

* * *

Harry was upset with Marianne who was still keeping company with Peterman Dave. Another companion had been brought in by one of his men. Though she was quite amusing, being the wife of a senior civil servant who spent time travelling and looking after his mistress, he resented the fact that Marianne was not in a hurry to return to him.

Charlotte de Matisse-Brinade was 41 years old and had been a silly woman. This had led to a series of illicit liaisons with people she did not know and would not normally associate with. Her current assignment servicing Harry Saunders was not the most unpleasant she had experienced. Nor was it the most enjoyable. Her husband was currently engaged in negotiation with the Lebanese Minister for

Trade, enjoying the hospitality of the Lebanese in Beirut.

Sitting in the lounge of the apartment in this rather run down area of the Paris suburbs was not her idea of fun. The indiscretion that had brought her to this situation had at least involved the hospitality of the Rue Haussmann, with the simple luxuries that went with it. She came out of her reverie and became aware of the conversation going on around her. Odd words impinged on her memory. Scraps of other conversations came back to her, creating a picture that did not please her at all. Stupid she may have been, but disloyalty to her country, was not one of her faults. She listened to the men laughing at the prospect of selling a weapon which had been made in Europe but that would be used to destabilize the French economy and that of the other Euro nations for the next ten years. The name of their customer frightened her. For the first time she began to realise that this was one encounter she may not survive.

She leaned against the window ledge and gazed out of the window desperately trying to think of a way she could get out of the apartment and perhaps into hiding. She heard the men leave, Harry's voice calling for them to join him at the club for a livener.

The door closed though she knew there would still be someone between her and the front door, there always was.

Her eyes roamed idly along the ledge outside the window. There was something in the corner that stirred a memory. Of course it was the reason she was in her present situation. She had been compromised by a bug, just like the one beside the window. That meant someone was listening to Harry's conversations. An enemy, perhaps. A rival? Maybe a way out for her?

"Whoever you are, I am trapped here. I can possibly be of help to you, if you can help me escape from this horrible situation. I will stand at this window at 2.00 pm and 4.00pm. Perhaps you could signal to let me know you have understood, and will help."

She stopped talking and started singing a little popular song as the minder came in.

"Who were you talking to, then?" He said rudely.

"I was singing to myself if you must know. There's no one here to talk to, is there?" She looked around the room to emphasise the point.

The man grunted, turned and went out again.

Charlotte looked at her watch 1.15pm. Her first contact time was 2.00 pm. She sat down and picked up one of the magazines from the coffee table and started to flit though the pages.

* * *

Donny picked up the message from Charlotte at 2.30pm. He arranged with Abby to cover the contact at 4.00 pm. They decided between them that the little laser key fobs that both carried would be suitable as a signal to contact Charlotte.

When Charlotte leaned against the inside window ledge at 4.00 pm Abby saw her and gave her a flash of the laser. Charlotte lifted her hand in acknowledgement.

The message came through that night at eight pm.

'Someone *called Peterman Dave had come through with the drawings. He will be meeting Harry to receive payment and make the handover at noon at the Orangery. Harry must be there in person and alone with the money to make the payment or the deal is off. Help me get out of this, please?*'

* * *

The arrangements planned for the Orangery were fairly straightforward. Donny and Abby in student guise would be there already looking at the Monet exhibition. Carol would be at the radio in the RV parked across the river. Jonathon would follow Harry into the Orangery, hopefully to watch the transfer, and with Donny and Abby manage the snatch.

Their only concern at this stage was the recovery of the drawings. The money and the two people involved were secondary. At this point. There would undoubtedly be Harry's men around the area. Abby would be given the recovered drawings to carry in the portfolio that many of the students of art carry, containing examples of their work. Donny would run interference. Jonathon would concentrate on Peterman and Harry if things worked out properly. All were very aware that plans only work if everyone does as expected. As Jonathon pointed out, "Things will go wrong. Think on your feet and act accordingly. Survive first, then the objectives."

Chapter Fifteen

The call came from Jonathon, as Donny and Abby left the Louvre where they had passed the time waiting to go to the rendezvous in the Orangery. Jonathon was held up in traffic and would not make it in time. Abby had answered the phone. "We are here. Don't worry. We'll manage. The crowds here make it easier for young people to get around without being noticed. Leave it to us." Though Jonathon was unhappy about it, there was nothing he could do. The matter was too important to let slide.

It was warm and sunny with a haze softening the hard edges of the Eiffel Tower overlooking the River. At the Orangery and the garden in which it stood, there were plenty of people about. Parties of tourists from the parked coaches followed the raised signs of their guides, motley crocodiles of people talking laughing and complaining.

Donny and Abby mixed happily with the crowd, drifting into the Orangery with a party of young people from Bulgaria.

All around the chatter of a multitude of languages assaulted their ears. Within the group they had joined there were several different dialects.

English, French and German were being used as the students themselves joked and insulted each other over their attempts to outdo each other.

Abby spotted two of Harry's men within moments of entering the gallery. Both stood out in the throng of tourists like sore thumbs. As she watched a casually-dressed woman went up to first one then the other. Whatever she said to them caused them both to edge their way out of the crowded room. She then stationed herself near the back of the room where she could keep an eye on the crowd.

Abby pointed her out to Donny. "Security, I reckon."

Donny agreed and indicated a small slim man who was looking over at the watcher from a place near the emergency exit. As they watched the woman looked at the man, who casually turned away without showing any interest.

There was a stir by the entrance as Harry pushed his way in looking thoroughly annoyed. He stood looking around the Gallery until his eye caught the man beside the emergency exit. He immediately began pushing his way through the crowd toward him. Donny and Abby looked at each other. They had discussed this between themselves before they came here today. Both turned and moving in different directions, they closed on the man they guessed was Peterman Dave. Donny reached him from behind. He stopped and waited until Abby was in position in front of their target.

Donny's fingers closed round the folder clutched tightly in Dave's hand without attempting to move it. Then Abby stumbled into Dave from the front, tripping gracefully so that her shoulder hit his solar plexus causing him to double up as the wind was knocked out of him.

She was all apologies as she grabbed him to help him keep his balance. As he struggled he lost his grip on the file in his hand. Donny caught it before it hit the ground. Opening the file and glimpsing the papers inside Donny stuck it inside his shirt. He shoved it down his waist band then keeping low he slipped through the crowd and left the Gallery. In the corner by the emergency exit the confusion became general, as Dave frantically searched for the missing file. Abby slipped away in the confusion and met up with Donny beside the ice cream vendor on the main street by the parked coaches. They struck up conversation with the collection of drivers waiting while their passengers saw the sights. Most of them were British. Together they watched the excitement at the Orangery as the crowd boiled out and two men were forcibly evicted by irate museum staff. The two heavies, who had been warned by the woman, stood about helplessly as they watched their boss manhandled by the museum staff. Then they both turned and made for their car parked up beside the road. As for Harry, he was icily furious. The case with the money was still in his hands.

With the drawings gone he was in trouble. The people he had promised them to were not the sort of people to disappoint.

Peterman Dave was not happy either as he left the gallery by the emergency exit setting off the alarm. By so doing, he caused even more confusion. When he met Marianne outside by arrangement, he explained what had happened.

Dave decided there were too many problems likely to arise from this debacle and turned to Marianne. "Honey, I need to finish this one way or the other. I need to stop Harry before he stops me. Understand?"

"I have a gun," was Marianne's answer. "Let's get on with it."

Donny and Abby were now beside the car, waiting for Harry to extricate himself from the attendants at the Gallery. Both the mob men who had come with Harry were at the car smoking. Donny slipped round the back of the Mercedes and stuck his penknife into the tyre. He signaled to Abby who pointed to the flat tyre and laughed. The two hoods were not amused. "Stupid cow!" One said and spat at her feet. Abby laughed even more and the other man started after her. His companion pointed at the flat and swore. He opened the boot and started lifting out the jack and spare to change the wheel.

His companion went to meet the irate figure of Harry, now nearly at the car carrying the case of money.

He looked at the flat tyre, opened the car door and sat in the driving seat. He lifted the car telephone.

Abby hit the man changing the tire with the tire-iron that was laying on the ground where he had taken it from the boot. He collapsed in a satisfactory manner and did not stir.

His companion saw her. Drawing his gun he suddenly stopped and looked unbelievingly at the red stain spreading on his shirt front. He gasped and fell down beside the car. Harry turned, and not seeing anyone, shouted, "Get round here one of you. I need you to ...." He stopped as he caught a glimpse of Donny, gun held close to his side turning his way. He reached for his own gun in the glove pocket of the car and actually had it in his hand, when Donny's bullet stopped everything. Donny's gun was suppressed. Thinking quickly he grabbed Harry's weapon and shoved his own into the slack hand of Harry Saunders. His body fell across the front seat of the car. He closed the door. Abby joined him.

They walked away hand in hand through the unknowing crowd.

Peterman Dave saw the whole thing. He also noticed that the case of money was still on the seat of the Mercedes. He strolled over to the car, ignored the two men lying on the ground, reached in through the car window and lifted out the case. Then he and Marianne left the area quietly arm in arm.

■■

Donny called Jonathon. He mentioned that there were vacancies in the Saunders organization and suggested that they should all meet at Harry's apartment to sort out the situation with Charlotte.

There was the usual heavy at the door, smoking and yarning with his partner, when Donny and Abby approached. Abby looked at the two men. Smiling, one said to the other "She's tasty and she looks up for it."

His companion laughed at him. "In your dreams, Pierre. She's class. Just winding you up."

Pierre was not amused and turned to Abby and Donny. "Hey, darling. Like to come in for a while?"

Abby smiled sweetly at him. "Yes. I think I would like that."

Pierre turned and looked triumphantly at his companion and opened the door. As he did so his companion collapsed, then he felt as if the roof had fallen on his head.

Abby put the tire iron away again. Having used it at the car it was still in her bag, appropriate for the present task.

Donny had used his gun butt just as effectively.

Holding the door open, he said. "Shall we?"

Jonathon arrived as they were about to enter the building. Looking at the two figures, he said. "I think they would be less conspicuous inside. Don't you?"

At the apartment door Abby knocked, while the others stood out of range of the spy hole. When the door opened they pushed their way in guns drawn.

The two men in the apartment were not really any trouble. Charlotte was released from her confinement as promised. They took the laptops and the hard drives from the computer and tied the two prisoners up. Jonathon suggested to them both that there were probably better healthier careers they could follow. They left them where they lay.

* * *

The last rays of the sun were glinting off the surface of the waters of the Mediterranean as Abby stretched luxuriously on the sunlounger.

Donny stepped out of the RV balancing a tray with tall glasses and a plate of snacks. He was followed by his father and Jonathon. The two men had come to meet Donny and Abby, here on the Mediterranean coast. Jonathon basically to confirm that the loose ends had all been tied up and the two young people could get on with their lives without having to watch their backs. Dan came simply to let them know that Mrs. Weston was recovering slowly and also to make sure that they were all right.

They all found chairs and sat down to enjoy the view in companionable silence.

As the evening show ended Jonathon asked, "What are you two going to do now? You took a year out and you still have nine months to go before you return to University."

Dan Weston laughed. "They have already worked that out, Jonathon. I believe they call this situation 'finding themselves' these days. In our day it was called dropping out. Whatever it is called we don't expect them to worry too much about work for the rest of the year.

Jonathon had a sudden vision of Carol smiling at him. "Tomorrow." He promised himself.

Dan looked at him quizzically?

"Nothing" Jonathon said with a small smile.

Later that night when they were alone once more, Abby said to Donny. "So what have you got planned for the rest of the year? I trust it will be something interesting."

Donny grinned "Oh, we'll think of something, I'm sure."

* * * * * * * *